MY MOTHER, MY CHAMPION

*Lessons and Inspiration from
My Mother's Story*

LORNA MAE JOHNSON

where words connect

MY MOTHER, MY CHAMPION

*Lessons and Inspiration from
My Mother's Story*

MY MOTHER, MY CHAMPION: *Lessons and Inspiration from My Mother's Story*

Copyright © 2024 Lorna Mae Johnson

ISBN: 978-1-959811-20-6 Paperback
ISBN: 978-1-959811-21-3 (eBook)

Library of Congress Control Number: 2023910406

Jacket design: Christine Pentagonias
Interior Design: Amit Dey
Editor: Winsome Hudson
Photos: Courtesy of the Author

Website: www.wordeee.com
Twitter.com/wordeeeupdates
Facebook: facebook.com/wordeee/
e-mail: contact@wordeee.com
Published by Wordeee in the United States, Beacon, New York 2024

Printed in the USA

Jamaica Map Outline

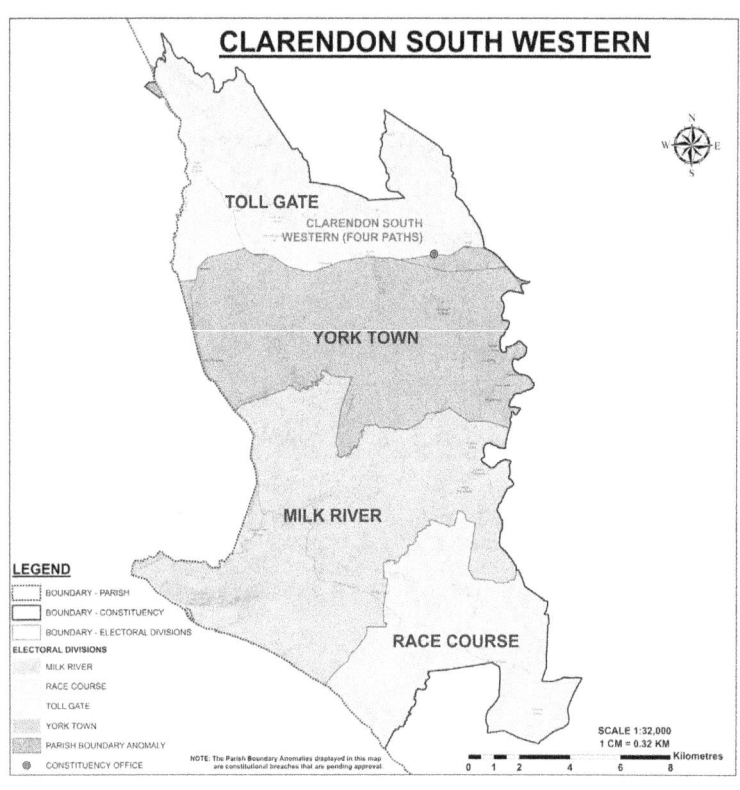

CLARENDON SOUTH WESTERN

TOLL GATE

CLARENDON SOUTH
WESTERN (FOUR PATHS)

YORK TOWN

MILK RIVER

RACE COURSE

LEGEND

BOUNDARY - PARISH
BOUNDARY - CONSTITUENCY
BOUNDARY - ELECTORAL DIVISIONS
ELECTORAL DIVISIONS
MILK RIVER
RACE COURSE
TOLL GATE
YORK TOWN
PARISH BOUNDARY ANOMALY
CONSTITUENCY OFFICE

NOTE: The Parish Boundary Anomalies displayed in this map
are constitutional breaches that are pending approval

SCALE 1:32,000
1 CM = 0.32 KM

Kilometres
0   1   2   4   6   8

In honor of my mother, sister and brother.
Proceeds from this book will help to fund the creation of a
Community Center to provide elder services and in support of
education for the youth of Clarendon.

ADVANCE PRAISE

"*My Mother, My Champion: Lessons and Inspiration from My Mother's Story* is a celebration of the formidable force that is a mother's love. Lorna Johnson unfolds a poignant and universal tale about her mother's determination to build a better life for her daughter—and how she forever serves as her daughter's guiding light. Through the story of Lorna and her extraordinary mom, girls around the world can get a glimpse of their limitless potential. I was personally moved to learn about the inspiration she has been to Lorna and to see how she continues to inform the leader that Lorna is today."

—*Representative Nancy Pelosi*
52nd Speaker of the House of Representatives

"I am honored to pay tribute to the remarkable woman who not only influenced the final stage of my athletic career but also touched the lives of countless others with her unwavering dedication and selflessness. Lorna, being a beacon of fortitude and discipline, set a positive example for me and some of my teammates, including the late Flo-Jo. This example radiated during our Olympic journey. Despite juggling a full-time job as a registered nurse and a rigorous training schedule, Lorna's determination and commitment as a teammate never wavered. Her selflessness and relentless pursuit of excellence undoubtedly influenced our success, culminating in Lorna achieving her best Olympic qualifying time of 11.4 seconds in the 100 meters, and my second gold medal victory in the 1988 Olympics. Lorna's resilience and work ethic exemplify the true spirit of a champion, making *My Mother, My Champion* a heartfelt tribute to her indomitable mother's enduring legacy. As the saying goes: "the apple doesn't fall far from the tree."

—Alice Brown,
2x USA Olympic Gold & Silver Medalist

"Often, we hear about how parents become a child's first teachers, guiding them through life's inevitable experiences. In LJ's beautifully written book about her mother, she pays a heartfelt tribute to the most extraordinary and inspiring teacher, mentor, and guiding light in her life. The wisdom her mother imparted, her uplifting spirit, and the profound bond they shared continue to resonate years after her mother's passing. Now, LJ lovingly shares this touching story with all of us in her inspiring book, *My Mother, My Champion.*"

—Anita McBride,
Chief of Staff to First Lady Laura Bush

"My Mother, My Champion: Lessons and Inspiration from My Mother's Story reflects the immeasurable power of ONE. I had the pleasure of collaborating with author, and entrepreneur, Lorna Mae Johnson, as we both shared a passion for mothers, child welfare/foster care.

Lorna's intrepid commitment and contributions toward women and children, mirror her elegant memoir, reminding us all that our histories matter. We must never forget to be authentic even if that makes us uniquely different from the rest. This book inspires readers to be courageous and pass forward the pricelessness of mentoring."

—Victoria Rowell, Actor
Bestselling Author, The Women Who Raised Me

"*My Mother, My Champion: Lessons and Inspiration from My Mother's Story* by philanthropist, businesswoman, and humanitarian Lorna Mae Johnson is a true testament to the effects of a loving, caring mother who offered invaluable lessons and guidance to her daughter.

Lorna's unique journey demonstrates the power of belief in oneself, her faith, and her determination to be of service to others. Her grace, her wisdom, and her humanity shine through as a source of hope and encouragement, and certainly her way of keeping the memories of her mom alive from the lessons she taught her. This is a very timely book that is authentic and refreshing. It will inspire readers to be the best that we can be."

—Dr. Pamela Appelt, Retired Judge
Court of Canadian Citizenship

"Our parents, mentors, champions, and other pivotal people who influence our outlook and make a difference in our experiences and outcomes are essential. As parents, our job is to nurture, protect, and inspire, and if we do it successfully, we leave footprints, even when we are no longer here.

As a mother, I am only glad that I was fortunate to have found so many whose templates for living provided valuable lessons and resources I can now pass on to my children. In my own story, my dear friend Lorna Johnson's book reminded me to assess with clear vision the people I embrace and those who surround me daily. I feel honored to be able to add my voice to Lorna and her family in recognizing a legacy of excellence. *My Mother, My Champion: Lessons and Inspiration from My Mother's Story* is a gem of a story of an amazing woman whose wingspan influenced the lives of many and whose story can be a source of strength and instruction to any reader wishing to write their own story. If a sense of purpose and direction is a part of your desire, *My Mother, My Champion: Lessons and Inspiration from My Mother's Story* will go a long way in helping you find your North Star. Embrace your success in the world."

—*Dame Tessy Anthony de Nassau*

"This is a story honouring one of the many unsung heroes of Jamaica, mothers who have touched the lives of many, turning these lives into great success stories, Rezna Ford Miller is one such mother. In this book, her daughter Lorna Johnson takes us on a remarkable journey of love, respect, and celebration of her life.

In every chapter her spirit of determination shines brightly, illuminating the paths she travelled and the countless hearts she touched, her life's journey is one of inspiration, through her trials and triumphs she exemplified the resilience of the human spirit and the power of determination. As we turn the pages of this book, let her story remind us of the extraordinary potential within each of us to make a difference in the world.

Etched in my memory is Rezna's resilience and grace, an enduring legacy that lives on in her children and grandchildren."

—*Odette Soberam Dyer, Regional Director*
Jamaica Tourist Board

xi

DEDICATION AND TRIBUTE

I am honored to have two most loving women
as my champions.

Rezna Bryan Ford
Known to me as Mama
Mentor
Hero
Remarkable Woman
When people tell me they admire my success,
my response is always the same,
"I'm my mother's daughter."

Ionie (Gem) McPherson,
My sister
My Encourager
My Motivator
My Best Friend
My Coach
She believed in me—always
and now her spirit lives in me.

AUTHOR'S NOTE

This book, like my mother, is complex and multilayered. In other words, a little bit of everything. Mainly, however, this is the story of my mother, a woman who was not only my champion but my guiding light to a bright future. The profound impact of her spirit, decisions, and internal drive on every life she touched still amazes me.

My mother was a special person who influenced others by example, moved others through support, and helped others through guidance and action. Her humility was respected, her accomplishments appreciated, and her lead-by-example philosophy was adopted by many. A strong woman with high character and steadfast morals, as Alzheimer's cast a shadow on her mind, I wanted her history, legacy, and heritage to endure. This book is my tribute to her, and a mentorship offering to those seeking inspiration to live vibrantly and share their unique gifts.

I am confident that my mother's story will help you discover your support system, influencing your journey in a meaningful way. This book, like my mother's lessons, is my vehicle, from walking on foot to a 'bicycle' and 'car' to traverse distant emotional landscapes. At its conclusion, find "Mama's Lessons" as takeaways—a blueprint to learn, reflect, and grow.

Questions stimulate thoughts, worksheets aid reflection, and I offer them freely, anticipating you'll soar as far as your wings can carry.

Like my mother, who lit my life on fire and helped me become the woman I am today, this book, I hope, will help you find your champion and the mentor who, though not necessarily family, will ignite your existence. I hope you enjoy *My Mother, My Champion: Lessons and Inspiration from My Mother's Story* as much as I enjoyed writing it.

With Inspiration,

Lorna Mae Johnson

FOREWORD

My Mother, My Champion
Lessons and Inspiration from My Mother's Story

A mother's love, at its best, is limitless. It is in so many ways the first and most perfect love and the principal way we come to understand our place in the world. Our mothers at their best are our most enthusiastic champions and our first teachers. They are also the pattern for who we one day could be.

Those of us who have been blessed to experience the unconscionable support of a loving mother know how that bond can imbue us with strength and build our character. We know it can be the rocket fuel that lifts us to the height of our dreams. When we are that lucky, we owe the universe real gratitude.

And that is the purpose of this book: to tell the story of a mother's unending love and support and how it inspired achievement and success in a young Jamaican girl with big dreams and in a community that needed to believe... This book is a letter of love and gratitude.

As an ambassador of change and of building community, Lorna Johnson has put to use invaluable lessons her mother taught her to build a stellar life for herself that has allowed her to impact her community in life-changing ways. *My Mother, My Champion: Lessons and Inspiration from My Mother's Story*, though a tribute to an indomitable woman, Johnson's mother, has universal appeal and will also serve as a mentorship guide for those who need someone to hold their space on the way to their North Star.

By the time the reader gets to the end of this great story, not only will they have learned about Jamaica and its culture, but they will also be inspired and motivated to live energetically, fearlessly, and ready to embrace all that life has to offer as they move steadfastly toward the vision they hold for their lives.

My story is similar to Lorna's in many ways and ultimately it was a story of will: the will to guide their children to achieve their dreams, while still pursuing theirs and finding meaningful ways to make life greater for the collective good.

Lorna, in this book, tells of her own journey as the daughter of a determined Caribbean mom, and how her mother's love and guidance shaped her. There's not a West Indian girl who won't recognize the women in this book and not a girl from anywhere in the world who won't see themselves and their own possibilities in Lorna and her extraordinary mom.

In short, this is a book about the power of "mother love."

Joy-Ann Reid
Host: *The ReidOut* on MSNBC
Twitter/IG:@joyannreid

Chapter One

TALLAWAH

*"Memory is a way of holding on to the things you love,
the things you are, the things you never want to lose."*

—*Kevin Arnold*

In the heart of Clarendon was a woman who defied conventions and commanded respect in her every stride. With her swinging hips and steady style, handbag over her wrist and a scarf tied under her chin, she was no ordinary person. She was what they called, "Tallawah." Tallawah is a Jamaican term that signifies a person who is a force of nature. This fierce spirit is innate to many island people for whom the term 'no problem' signifies their laid-back nature but when faced with challenges, *their inborn fierceness* takes over. Perhaps their indomitable spirit is fueled by a mix of the blazing sun and the hypnotic, lulling beauty of the tropical paradise. This is the land in which my mother, possessing the spirit of a titan, stood tall. Mama, my champion, was a Renaissance woman ahead of her time.

Jamaica, the land of wood and water with its majestic mountains, crystalline seashores, and endless blue sky, is where you'll find Clarendon and some of the fiercest people on the island. The third-largest parish in the middle of the island, fifty-three kilometers from its capital Kingston, and equidistant from its most westerly end, Negril, spawned many *Tallawah* people who went on to world fame: the prolific writer, Claude McKay; sixties pop sensation singer Millie Small, *My Boy Lollipop*; reggae superstar Toots Hibbert of Toots and the Maytals and their unforgettable 1966 Festival song, *Bam, Bam*; adopted sprinter, the legendary Merlene Ottey, nine-time Olympic medalist with fourteen World Championships and seven World Indoor Championships to her credit, and Leonard P. Howell, the founder of the Rastafarian movement. Clarendon's Mocho, Bull Head Mountains, and the Rio Minho River were long used to serving up quality people, and my mother, born in the parish, was indeed *tallawah* and certainly a woman of substance.

Rezna Bryan, also known as "Mama" and "Miss Girly," was born August 14, 1931, and grew up in Corn Piece, then, a rural enclave as it remains today, near the parish capital May Pen where people in the community looked out for each other.

The thirties and forties were challenging times for the people of Jamaica, shaping the outlook of many rebel spirits. Discontent from the fallout of the Great Depression, made worse by the fact that Emancipation had not delivered on the promise of a better life, spurred great unrest. Long used to fighting for their rights, Jamaicans held to the prophetic words of Delroy Wilson that "better mus come." Bob Marley would later echo these sentiments in his own song, "Get Up, Stand Up."

Many have said that the fighting spirit of Jamaicans was inherited from our ancestors—the Gg people brought from the Gold Coast of Ghana to the island as slaves. Upon landing, many of these warriors escaped to the mountains. They came to be known as the Maroons and were never enslaved. One such was a woman guerilla fighter, Nanny of the Maroons who led countless insurrections against the British in the 1800s. Every time I look at her picture, I am reminded of my mother's indomitable spirit. Nanny was no joke.

By the 1930s, workers, fed up with the poor working conditions under the British, led a strike at the Crown's "goldmine," the West Indies Sugar Company (WISCO), in Frome, Westmoreland. This insurrection exploded into an island-wide uprising that lit the country on fire and inspired workers' strikes throughout the entire Caribbean. While Haiti had long been known for its fierceness against the French, the vocal and revolutionary islanders of Jamaica, the third largest of the islands, 90 miles from Cuba where a young Fidel Castro would later lead another revolution, now set the standard, not only in the Caribbean but worldwide, as "no-nonsense, fearless people."

The 30s and 40s were times of radical change. The prevailing message of self-government and self-love by Jamaicans like Marcus Garvey went far and wide, even reaching the Black Mecca of Harlem, USA. Whether Mama's personality was formed by this revolutionary period or passed down from her parents who'd lived through these radical times, she was a self-determined child who became a self-determined woman.

As significant landowners the Bryans were considered "privileged" and lived a comfortable life by rural Jamaican standards. Mama's large family dated back generations. The family's land wealth was passed down from my grandfather Uriah's father. How great grandpa got his lands was most probably from colonial government purchases during the time of land redistribution. Less likely is that it was captured land when slave owners fled the island.

Upon Grandpa Uriah's parent's death, his children inherited his properties. The girls Aida, Sarah, and Ethel were landowners. Mama's dad Uriah, and his brothers, Ernest, and Claudie, were true entrepreneurs and expanded the family's fortune. Their other brother, Isaiah was never involved in the family business and seems to have simply disappeared. It was rumored that some of Grandpa's family had immigrated to Cuba to work in the sugar factories but not all of them returned to Jamaica. Still, no one knew what happened to Isiah and not much was said about him. Let's say he was a lost sheep.

In addition to running a prosperous tobacco farm, the strapping, good-looking brothers controlled the area's sugarcane production, the butchery, and even the distribution channel—horse carts to transport sugar cane and other goods to their destination. They raised horses, donkeys, cows, goats, chickens, and other farm animals, expanding their ever-growing businesses. And Mama acquired the same entrepreneurial skills.

It's hard to say whether this was naturally inborn or because she'd borne the burden of loss and grief too often and too early in life because Mama always had a special wit and way about her. The first of Mama's many losses started with her mother's death before she'd turned the age of ten. Nobody knew what caused Grandma's death; she just died. Grandpa, Uriah Bryan, and Grandma, Curdel Brightly each came from prominent families in the area and both had children from previous relationships.

After Grandma's passing, Grandpa Uriah, still in love with his wife, never married again (though he later had another child, a boy named Lynton, whom he brought home to be raised with the girls, so he must have had love affairs), leaving Mama and her two younger sisters, Mavis, and Gertrude, in that order, without a mother. It had to be hard for children so young to grow up without a mother, but Jamaica is not a society that dwells in 'navel-gazing or woe is me' psychology, and as such, life simply had to go on. The children had to adjust in whatever way they could. Though Grandpa Uriah's brother's wife, Violet Fullerton, stepped in to assist, no one could ever replace their mother.

Mama Finds Her Voice

Left to her devices, the independent Rezna learned to listen to her own voice, which in 1946, at the age of fifteen, led her to follow a young Pentecostal missionary named Eunice Knight, who was sent to Corn Piece to convert the dwellers to the word of God.

To the British, their colonies' heathens needed to find God so in 1815, missionaries arrived in Jamaica. Anglican and Roman Catholic churches were erected, ready to convert the islanders. The first Pentecostal church was founded in 1933, in Kingston by none other than the father of the world-renowned superstar, Grace Jones. With its emphasis on a personal experience of God through baptism, Pentecostalism was a religion of the people. It was also the first religion on the island that gave women the opportunity to be ordained as preachers. Though Rastafarianism was founded around the time of Mama's birth and was rooted in African beliefs and celebrated the Black Redeemer, Haile Selassie of Ethiopia (the only country on the African continent never enslaved), truer to

Mama's disposition was the comfort she felt in a religion that spoke to her spirit.

Though she had no wish to be a minister, at sixteen, Mama was baptized at the Church of God of Prophecy and joined hands with her spiritual teacher, Eunice Knight whom I came to know as Evangelist Smith. A true believer, Evangelist Smith, the charismatic twenty-one-year-old, full of conviction and promise of prosperity for all, influenced Mama to help start a new church in the area.

"Rezna, I know it's hard to choose, but heed the Lord's scriptures. Jeremiah 29:11 says, "For I know the plans I have for you, plans to prosper you and not harm you, plans to give you hope and a future."

Mama believed in her vision.

"*But is wah dis nonsense mi hearing 'bout Mis Girly? She a go do wah?*" the village rumor mill was in full swing. The adage 'it takes a village' was real back then, and the villagers had an opinion on Mama's far-from-expected decision.

"*No Sah, it caan bi true. No way whatsoever.*"

No matter what people tried to say to Mama, she was stubborn and had a mind of her own. She knew her 'why'—her purpose in life very early on and when it came to executing her vision for *her* life, her faith was non-negotiable.

"This is my calling, and I have to obey," Mama would reply. In Mama's mind, serving a higher purpose was to be the jewel in her everlasting crown. Her belief was that service to people less fortunate than herself would be best served through Christ and given the grinding poverty around her, she felt the need to help, especially children. To her, a well-lived life required purpose, and hers was to be in faith and of service.

Mama's resolve was eventually accepted and embraced by the community, but not so fast within the Bryan household.

"You *waan do wah*?" Grandpa Uriah would square his shoulder and puff on his cigar as if to say this conversation was over. But Mama cleaved to her scriptures reciting 1 Corinthians 2:5, "That your faith might not rest in the wisdom of men but in the power of God." And with that, she defied her father.

Life would have been far easier had Mama taken the expected path and gotten involved in the family businesses. However, the path mapped out for her by her family did not fit her personality one bit and she railed against such conformity. Mama began butting heads with her father. What's more, her brilliant, sharp, and visionary mind saw opportunities when others couldn't, and she acted on those instincts causing even further strife.

Her father vehemently objected. Mama couldn't understand why he was so against her decision to serve the Lord when she was doing good things. After all, the community of Corn Piece was one in which the Lord was no stranger! Guinness Book of Records notes that there are more churches in Jamaica per square mile than anywhere else in the world, and Corn Piece was no exception!

The more Grandpa objected; the more Mama rebelled. Finally, Mama opted to leave behind her cushy life to strike out on her own. It was a big deal to drop out of high school back then, as education, free from ages three through fifteen, was still for the privileged few. But Colonial education, with its cooking and sewing classes to prepare girls for menial jobs and as wives, didn't mesh with Mama's calling any more than taking her place in the family business. She was far too independent to be a follower of anything or anyone not suited to her purpose.

So, Mama decided that since she was not going to finish school and had no intention of taking her place in the family business, she would find work to support herself and fulfill her dream of starting a church alongside Evangelist Knight in Corn Piece.

"Girly, *yu* not making any sense. *Yu* almost graduating. The Lord *caan* wait on you to build this church till after *yu* graduate," her sister Mavis said.

It was no use. No one could talk Mama out of her decision, even as close to graduating as she was. Some turned a blind eye while others grumbled under their breath. Mama, not in the habit of concerning herself with what other people thought, or letting her ego get in the way, kept to her plan. She simply carried on.

Mama began doing menial jobs to become financially independent—running errands, selling our Aunt Sa Vie's readymade clothes, and doing other kinds of work no one else thought to do. Her work ethic, regardless of what she could find to do, became the talk of the town, and through word of mouth, her business quickly grew.

"But *dat Girly* no easy. She *suppun'* else," the townspeople exclaimed. "She is definitely her own person. Imagine a girl from a *'fambily'* like that doing the kind of things she *'doin'.*"

From Mama's earnings, some of which she gave to erecting a place of worship, she, and Evangelist Smith started the church (Church of God of Prophecy). In respective ways, they dedicated themselves to building a flock for Jesus. While Mama built her business, Evangelist Smith tended to the day-to-day needs of the church, which soon began to sprout. The naysayers flocked to see what was happening over at Mama's church (some people actually called it Sister Ford's church).

"But *dat Girly* really no easy," they'd say again and again.

The church developed and rapidly grew in membership. Mama and Evangelist Smith had to find bigger quarters to host their gatherings. Though she owned land her father had given all his children, Mama's independent streak wouldn't allow her to utilize it for a project to which he objected. It was a quandary. But again, Mama, not the kind to look back or have regrets, looked for another solution which arrived in the form of my grandaunt, Sarah Bryan. My grandpa's sister came to the rescue and gave them a place to hang their hats right there, in front of her house. Their first real church, made from wattle and coconut bows was built. They called it 'ThachieMini.'

Not seeing eye-to-eye with her father didn't prevent Mama from communicating with her family and when her aunt came to her support, they rallied. She remained close to her brothers and sisters, from both her father's and mother's side, with no distinction ever drawn between them. They were a tight-knit family. Mama even began encouraging them to join the church.

Finding Solutions

Privileged or not, rural Jamaica in the mid-1940s had no electricity. As with all of Mama's enterprises, solving community needs created business opportunities. She began burning wood to make coal to sell. The coal was also the dawn of the sweet potato pudding I'd come to love. Made in a dutchie pot with coal on top and bottom, the custard, a soft gooey layer forming on top of that 'pone,' was what we called heavenly.

Day by day, Mama's businesses grew. The new talk of the town was now this: "*Respeck* due, man. That woman *suppin'* else for real. She done turn into a real 'chiney man'.

Seven ethnic groups make up Jamaica. With its mishmash of nationalities it soon became a multicultural nation with all cultures seamlesly existing together. Now mixed up, all are considered Jamaicans. Thus, our motto: "Out of Many One People." The six hundred thousand stubborn Blacks who were forcibly brought there as a result of the transatlantic slave trade, first arrived on the banks of the Rio Minho River in the very parish of Clarendon on the Spanish boats, the Niña, Pinta, and Santa Maria. The Italian Christopher Columbus had captained the fleets on expeditions for Queen Isabella and King Ferdinand of Spain. These African slaves were meant to farm tobacco on the island for the Spanish Empire and brought their own vibrant cultures, and the Spaniards were no match for them.

By the time the British came, tired of the obstinate Africans, most Spaniards had long fled the island, abandoning their plantations. With the constant rebellion of these most obstreperous people, post-Emancipation, the British imported indentured servants such as the Chinese and East Indians to replace the rioting and warring slaves; however, these groups were more inclined to commerce.

The Chinese, mainly of Hakka descent, arrived on the island in 1854 from Panama, China, and the East Indians even before. Many started their lives with nothing, but with hard work and sacrifice amassed great wealth within a few years. The Chinese especially flourished, owning almost every grocery store on the island. Ironically, to this day, many Jamaicans use Chin to mean all Chinese, just as they do Cutex to mean all nail polish and tea to mean breakfast. When they say they're going shopping at Mr. Chin's, there is no guarantee that the shop owner's family name is actually Chin. They could be Lees, Hosangs, Changs, or Chungs. Mr. Chin means a Chinese shop even if the sign over the door clearly says Mr. Hosang's General Store.

Later, other nationalities, such as the Lebanese and Syrians, came to the island seeking freedom from persecution. Just as the Chinese dominated the grocery stores, the haberdasheries were owned by the Lebanese, and the jewelry businesses by the Indians. Commerce on the island was often operated by these 'imported' people, but because of her commercial success, Mama became an honorary Chinese merchant, and was often referred to as a "chiney man."

Mama found great success in the coal business, making enough money to start her second business, buying fabric and selling it throughout the neighborhood. Her immediate client reach, too limited on foot for Mama's ambition inspired her next solution, to become mobile. She bought a bicycle and began traveling farther and farther away as a materials supplier. As her reach expanded, so did her profits and the growth of her church. Again, realizing her limitations on her bike, Mama purchased a car, a green Austin Cambridge station wagon with a brown wood panel. That was a big deal in our community. It was the only car owned by anyone, male or female, in the area, let alone the community. A woman titan was born! The community again chimed in. "Yes, Lord, that Girly is one *Tallawah* woman."

Now a formidable competitor for the Chinese and Indian families who ran most of the businesses in the area, Mama was one of a small group of privileged pure-blood Black women to own a business on the island of Jamaica. She truly seemed unstoppable.

Knowing what it felt like to have a burning passion, to be different, Mama went out of her way to accept people for who they were, and so was beloved by her community and embraced by the other merchants. Yet, the irony of it all was that Mama did not escape the rampant classism in Jamaica. "Because I care for you doesn't mean you could sit at the table for Sunday dinner," colored her philanthropy with a tinge *oblige noblesse*—the inferred responsibility of the privileged to act with generosity in taking care of the less fortunate. In hindsight, Mama herself held classist views, a colonial leftover that everyone embraced, and to be forthright, had its advantages, especially when it came to setting expectations back then. Everybody accepted their roles without question, which made for an orderly society, and home was no different. Subsequently, labor and social upheavals would change the dynamics of Jamaica's social structure.

Chapter Two

TITAN

*"Power without compassion is like a giant
that blocks the sunlight."*

—Criss Jami, *Healology*

As Mama's businesses grew, so did her travels, leaving little room for romance with the young men from our neighborhood. Any spare moment not spent working was devoted to building her church membership. At the crack of dawn, Mama would pack up her car with goods, embarking on her journey to service her numerous clients long before the roosters crowed. It was during her travels across the island, when she was about eighteen, that she met my father, Noel Augustus Johnson, from Catadupa, in the parish of St. James, its bustling capital, Montego Bay.

A lively tourist hub, far more vibrant a city than the quiet Corn Piece, Montego Bay stood as the premier traveler's destination, serving as a vital pillar of the Jamaican economy. The 1950s witnessed Montego Bay and Ocho Rios's tourism flourishing, but it was the early 1960s that ushered in what came to be known as the Golden Age of Tourism. Travelers could not get enough of the land of adventure: its lush vegetation, serene landscapes, vibrant sunset, pristine turquoise waters, and endless stretches of white sandy beach. Jamaica, in turn, reveled in the influx of tourist dollars, offering unparalleled service and style that attracted avant-garde celebrities like Peter O'Toole, Sophia Lauren, Errol Flynn, Audrey Hepburn, and Ian Fleming, whose James Bond 007 film, *Dr. No*, was partially filmed on his estate, Goldeneye. And who could forget Ursula Andress rising out of the deep, blue Caribbean Sea in a white bikini? The tourists who were frequent visitors even had homes on the island.

Meeting Her First Love

Undoubtedly, Papa, a railroad train conductor, encountered people of different nationalities and cultures who traveled to the island by rail. A suave transplant from Mobay, as Montego Bay is locally known, a man with a cosmopolitan outlook would certainly have matched Mama's broad perspective on life, and she found herself captivated by his charm. Catadupa, St. James, where my father was born, was nothing like Mobay. It was truly country. So country, even their language sounded different from Clarendonians. But Papa had long been 'international' because his work necessitated him traveling the island. Perhaps when he met Mama, he was drawn to the composed demeanor of this tall, quiet, attractive, and independent woman with the earnest qualities of a Catadupa woman. More attractive to him than the "fast women" city dwellers, he was smitten with Mama, and Mama, a Corn Piece woman, found herself drawn to his worldly demeanor." After a whirlwind courtship, Mama brought Noel Augustus Johnson to Corn Piece, Hayes near her old home, where they set down roots and began their life together. *"Well, it look like God has been shining his light on Girly fi true! She catch a good country man."* The village choir chimed in.

Jamaican culture, formed on the back of British culture, is decidedly British with rituals, mores, and hand-me-down ideals. It was not uncommon when local Jamaicans came from Kingston, the island's capital, Montego Bay or Ocho Rios, to Clarendon that the uppity ones thought of Corn Piece as country and backward. The "speakie spokie," condescending people, as we would call them; those who sounded and behaved more British than the Queen of England, would refer to us Clarendonians as bush people, much like our friends from Hayes called us when we moved to Uppa Hill. Bush yes, because it wasn't yet built up but it was neither country nor backward. No! Uppa Hill may have been far from the main road, but it was a lush, remote haven with stunning sunrises, sunsets, and a vibrancy that was great for a visionary like Mama. The class-conscious people had no problems looking down their noses on those less fortunate, their behavior was sometimes more oppressive than the masters they drove out.

Though Papa was a laborer, he must have been accepted as Mama's equal as people decided not to interfere. Neither the townspeople nor her sisters posed any objection. After all, Mama had delivered on every promise she'd made to herself and had made her community proud.

Not long after he moved to Hayes, Papa and Mama bought a piece of land together and built a house. With its red shingled tin roof, white-washed exterior, and barbed wire fences, the two-bedroom house sat on acres of land. Dotted with fruit trees offering their goodies: jackfruit, dwarf mangoes, sweetsop and soursop, tamarind, coconut, ackee, banana, and one of my favorites, Julie mango, it was a haven. On either side of the walkway, hedges of mango rose flowers and marigolds led up to the verandah. The large living and dining areas were merged, and later, Mama even built a garage for her beloved Austin Cambridge. In those days, homes had outdoor latrines and kitchens because, as with electricity, plumbing had yet to arrive in Hayes. Nighttime outdoor trips to the bathroom are stories all by themselves.

Building the house was a big deal and a highlight for Mama and Papa. They were in love. They were happy. Mama though had inherited the stiff upper lip of the British so she was not a woman of many emotions or words. Still, everyone knew how much she loved Papa. As powerful a woman as Mama was, she took the best care of her husband, and her role as a wife and mother who at first had to cook and clean was no affront.

Even when Papa came in under his "waters," she never said a word, instead offering honey water. Papa wasn't the only Jamaican man who came home to his wife drunk. It seemed many Jamaican men had a penchant for stopping at rum bars on their way home from work, especially on payday Fridays. Still, they were happy, and it was in this house that their last two children were born, Judith and me. It always tickles me looking back at our birth dates that most of us kids were born on the 21st day of our particular month Ionie and I on January 21st and Warren on November 21st. Judith, born December 10th was the exception, which of course, was portending.

Staying home more did not mean Mama was home every day. As her work as a businesswoman was demanding, Mama had a maid and a yard boy to assist her in taking care of the house. She was still gone a lot doing her business all over the island even though we were young. She finally called her sister.

"Girty," she'd implored, "I have so much work and have to be gone a lot. I really don't like the children being home just with the helper (housemaid) and you know Noel. Would you come and look after them while I take care of the business?"

With that, Mama employed her younger sister Gertrude (Aunt Girty), with whom she was very close, as our nanny. Aunt Girty assumed Mama's duties while the helper managed the household. We also had the support of the gardener, who kept the hedges trimmed and whitewashed the tree trunk with limestone to protect the sprouting shrubs. And, of course, we had the empowered "village people" who would 'tell' our mother if we got out of line.

We loved Aunt Girty. Unfortunately, when we were still relatively young she migrated to England. The distressing times lingered well into the 50s for island folk after the Great Depression and so a decimated Britain passed the British Nationality Act of 1948 giving British nationals full British citizenship. Advertisements to the colonies began appearing, promising cheap transportation, and a better life with vast opportunities for advancement and work. As a result, 492 Jamaicans landed in Tilbury, Essex, on the HMT Empire Windrush in 1948 to help rebuild the 'motherland.' This was the beginning of a mass exodus of our people to foreign lands, mainly to England in the earlier years, and the beginning of England's multiculturalism.

With ships coming back and forth from 1945 to the 1960s to take passengers to England, Aunt Girty left in search of better opportunities. The day before she left, we stayed up all night. It was like a send-off party. It would be a long, grueling boat trip of almost twenty-two days before Aunt Girty would arrive in the motherland, and we wouldn't see her again for years. Mama, four years older, and Aunt Girty, were the best of friends, and in a sense, this was another loss for Mama.

When we were still quite young, Mama built a grocery shop in front of our house. This meant she could be home more. Not one to spare the rod, it also meant we children might catch more of her sternness. There was a constant flow of traffic at the store. I used to love watching the people going and coming with their requests.

"*A pound a flour and a quarter pound of saltfish. Yu have cooking h'oil this week?*"

"*A tin a bully beef and some grater cake.*"

Mama and her helpers would be forever chopping salt fish, weighing flour and sugar on the hand scale hanging from the ceiling, and putting them in paper bags for her customers. Along with the staples, there was often a bottle of syrup, sardines, and a bag of water crackers. The grocery store became the village social spot with people milling around, chatting about politics and religion, or hanging out drinking Guinness stout and sodas. Mama would knock back a stout now and then, preferring to think of it as tonic rather than the liquor her faith disallowed.

We were all school age now, even Judith, as Jamaican children start school at three years old. By now, we had moved to Uppa Hill, and our new helper, Sister Ormsby, who lived next door, would arrive at about 6 a.m., just about when our barnyard rooster would start crowing his head off. Early, with the morning dew still on the ground, we'd hear dutchie pots banging around. Sister Ormsby was getting ready to cook breakfast. Shortly after, we'd smell the aroma wafting through our windows. Warren's day would be made if breakfast included fried dumplings.

The crowing of the rooster would spur us into action, and we'd jump out of bed and turn on the radio singing along to, "*If you see the rooster running sixteen sexy chickens chasing him, he's balling for murder*" as that song was the first song played on the radio every morning. Then it was a whirlwind of activities as we dashed to get ready for school. We'd quickly "wash up," having taken our baths the night before when sister Ormsby, always prepared, would wash us in the big tub under the outdoor pipe or spray us down with the hose. We'd lather nice and sudsy with Castile soap and then jump into the tub of water or run through the hose frolicking, carefree, coming out squeaky clean. Indeed, right after dinner, she'd be waiting for us, and we loved it.

In the morning, after our 'wash up', it was time for us girls to get our hair braided in plaits; five, three, or two cornrows before we'd don our pleated blue uniforms with its sparkling white blouse and red tie.

"Everybody ready," Mama would call out if she was home.

"Yes." We'd chime in chorus.

"Good. Then come, let me see you." She'd inspect us to make sure we were properly dressed, our hair neatly combed and tied with a ribbon, and our underwear clean and in good repair.

"Okay, everybody look good. Off you go. Don't forget to walk on the right side of the road and look out for each other, you hear." My mother never said, "I love you." Not until we were grown, by which time we'd found a devilish way to pry the words from her lips by staying on the phone and refusing to get off until she actually said the words. Though rarely spoken, Mama's love was a love you felt, took comfort in, and knew it came in many forms: the gentle touch, the gleaming eyes, and even the rod of correction.

"We won't, Mama."

Our uniforms, starched and ironed until the pleats were sharp like a blade, could almost walk by themselves. At school, we'd even created a starched uniforms competition—to see who had the sharpest pleats. So, every night we'd put more starch on the uniform and iron it for the next day's razor-sharp and stiff-as-a-board look as we'd head out.

In his khaki uniform and red tie, my big brother Warren would lead the way to school. Like little lambs we held hands sometimes to protect each other, walking on the left side of the road on the way to school and the right side home (Jamaicans drive on the left, and according to Mama, we must always be going in the direction of oncoming traffic). Our every move was scrutinized once beyond our homestead, and we were not always quite so lamblike, though we kept on our best behavior. We didn't like it when the villagers interfered by giving Mama a bad report when she returned from a trip, and believe me, if we broke that rule news traveled very fast, even in a community with no telephones.

Bartering: The Art Of Business

As was customary in Jamaica at that time, Mama did a lot of bartering with people who worked for her. Her suppliers, understanding the need to manage cost and profits were more than happy to comply. Mama was an outstanding negotiator too. I was awed every time I watched Mama make a deal. Generous but firm, when she was done, everyone walked away feeling empowered and satisfied. Rather than simply creating an empire for herself and her family, Mama saw her success as a means to help others, and she schooled many in the art of business. At an early age, Mama's life began leaving an imprint on who I would become. I wanted to walk in her footsteps, and I vowed that one day I would make her proud.

Visiting Gong Gong

To make sure we got to know the other side of our family, for the summers, we were sent to visit Papa's mother in Catadupa. By car, when Mama drove us, it would take four long hours. It felt like the other side of the world to us kids. When Mama couldn't drive us to "country," however, the train was efficient and fun, and our much-preferred mode of transportation. Jamaica's railroad, constructed in 1845, was the second British colony after Canada to get a railway system. The hour-plus-long train ride made travel to other communities easier and more efficient, and spending time in the country with Grandma, whom we called Gong Gong, made for special times.

Our big adventure was chaperoned by our brother Warren. Being the oldest, he was put in charge, and it was exciting as Warren was a hoot. We felt like grown-ups. And even then I suspected Mama was comfortable sending us alone since Papa had worked for the transportation authority, and the conductors would likely look out for us.

I *loved* riding the train. I was always delighted when it pulled into a stop, and the vendors rushed to the windows peddling their goods.

"*Shrimps, Middle quarters shrimps,*" They'd push their plastic bags of goodies through the windows. There were drops, roasted peanuts, and peppered shrimp, so hot, it had the water spilling from our eyes! There were also the stops where we could buy bags of juicy oranges. I knew all of the twenty stations by heart and would read them off until the next stop would be Catadupa Station: May Pen, Forth Park, Clarendon Park Station,…Maggotty Station,…Ipswich Station. At Catadupa we'd be ready to jump off at our stop as the train never lingered long in any station.

When we arrived at Catadupa, there was still a long walk, about a one-mile trek to get to Grandma's house. Jokester that he was, Warren would sometimes jump back onto the moving train and hang off the edge, waving. He would then jump off again before the train sped up. We made a game out of everything, not appreciating the danger of our play. Ionie (whom we called Gem), Judith, and I would walk on the train rail to see how long we could balance ourselves, it sometimes became a serious competition. We would also hop back and forth onto the tracks like we were playing hopscotch and we would also run and race each other from one point to the next. These are some of the things we did to pass the time until we got to the bottom of the hill where Gong Gong lived. That hill seemed like a humongous mountain. I'd muster all my energy to make the climb. Gong Gong was always looking forward to seeing us and she would be waiting at the top of the hill with open arms and had drinks prepared for us. It would either be sugar and water with lime (lemonade in the U.S.) or Kool-Aid.

"My children," she'd spread her arms, and we'd all run to hug her, then each trade her a refreshing drink for the gifts Mama always sent along. Gong Gong often said that my mom, Girly, was her favorite daughter-in-law.

Catadupa was so rural, that we called where my grandma lived the "country country," much like the Kingston people called Corn Piece the backlands. The island's local dialect, *Patois* is a mix-up like its people; broken English, French, Spanish, Latin, and various West African languages and was understood island wide, but I swore the people of Catadupa spoke a different language. The language Grandma spoke seemed more authentic to our African roots and I would strain and train my ears to understand it.

The immense property Gong Gong owned had a modest house built on stilts, with a large veranda. Grandma's rocking chair on one side was where she would smoke her pipe and puff her cigar at the end of her day and enjoy the evening breeze. Grandma's home had a cellar, the perfect place to play hide and seek. Never too old, she would join us as we darted off to find ideal hiding spots. We also looked forward to meeting up with our other cousins, who also visited Grandma for the summer. It was like going to summer camp. All summer, we helped Gong Gong on her farm where acres and acres of seasonal fruit trees grew abundantly: mangoes, pear (avocados), yams, coconuts, sour lime (which I loved), and star apple among them. It never seemed like a chore to us as we helped to gather the harvest.

Apart from my father, who often visited his mother before he got sick, Grandma had six other children. My father's brother, Uncle Papa was never around because he'd gone to England. I only remember my Aunt Nellie and her husband who lived with Gong Gong and helped her on the farm, and my Aunt Vera with her deep voice that I later learned I was blessed with. They would come by to gather the crop to sell at the market, as this was how they supported themselves and Grandma. We'd make quite a dent in the merchandise, eating our way through all the fruits we could. It was fun and different, and we thoroughly enjoyed everything we did with grandma. We even put aside goodies from the "country country" to take back home for Mama.

My fondest memory in Catadupa was going to *Gong Gong's* church Pukkumina (pocomania), or revivalist church. A derivative religion with deep African roots, the Great Revival, as it was called, was brought over in the 1860s during the days of slavery. It is a mixture of Christian, protestant, and other European beliefs, and Sundays at Grandma was an experience. The congregation, dressed in long, colorful outfits, heads tied with a turban, would feverishly dance to the percussion drums' deep, rhythmic sounds. Hot and humid, Chinese fans would be furiously wafting the still air as women fanned themselves. I'd sit close to them to get the breeze of the fans.

When the pastor took the pulpit, the congregation would raise their voices in *Amen* and *Praise the Lord* as the zealous preacher effortlessly waxed his sermon and cast out demons. The more fervent the sermon, the more bodies would begin gyrating. Fans were abandoned as parishioners thrashed around raising their voices in *Hallelujah,* exulting, and glorifying the Most High. Then, when filled with the holy ghost, they would succumb to the spirit and begin speaking in tongues, sweat drenching their spirit-filled bodies.

The church's belief is in a direct relationship with the Almighty. This was considered an affront to the Crown and the religious hierarchy. As such, the vexed royalists falsely derided the religion, making it synonymous with Obeah—in their mind, an occult belief and devil-worshiping ritual. For me, it truly was a celebration, and I enjoyed every minute of it. I would join in doing the Pukkumina dance, which I loved. My body swayed hypnotically, surrendering to the beauty of the moment. I became so good at my reenactment of the dance that I won many awards for school performances. At home, I would practice in front of Mama, and she'd be tickled. The more she laughed, the harder I danced. It was a joyous time.

Chapter Three

Sundays were a special day for us. Like clockwork, it meant church, Sunday School, and family visits. Our church was lively although not as spirited as Grandma's. After services ended, the congregation would sometimes gather to eat, drink, catch up on the latest news, and make merry before it was time to go home. As children, we loved hanging out to play with other kids. My father wasn't much of a churchman so I don't remember him being with us at church or on family visits. My memories of him are sketchy at best because he was ill most of our young years—in and out of the hospital all the time. I do remember once him picking me up, throwing me up in the air and catching me then bringing me to his chest as he laid on his back and I chuckled. Another time, when he came home from the hospital and attempted to pick me up I cried and ran away, and my mother tried to get me to go back to him so he could hold me.

The only other memory I have is of one Sunday when Mama was going to church, warning us she was about to leave us behind to walk so she wouldn't be late. Whether she wanted us along or not, I suspect it was more for his own sake than for hers, perhaps wanting the place to himself, but Papa quickly helped us get dressed in our pink and blue frilled bottom dresses and put us in the car. I remember that Sunday very vividly as we had fun trying to get dressed quickly and him picking us up one by one and putting us in the back of the green station wagon. Those are the few memories of my father that I cherish. After meeting my father's younger brother, whom we call Uncle Papa, later in life, he rekindled my memory of my father as they looked so much alike.

I want to be able to tell you how handsome my father was and how sturdy and loving, but I can't because I don't remember much about him. From what I understood, he might have been an alcoholic because one of the complications of his illness was liver problems. It was said that Papa had a flirtatious personality, a common trait among Jamaican men. Eventually, rumors circulated in the community choir that he was a bit of a playboy. However, Mama paid little attention to such gossip, though infidelity was common in Jamaican society, possibly inherited from our African ancestors' polygamous traditions or from plantations' socioeconomic practice of breeding enslaved families for profit. Unlike many, my dad had no other children outside of his marriage to my mom, except his first son long before he'd met Mama. He was a committed and devoted husband.

With the freedom to travel the island by train, Papa probably could have had a girlfriend at each station, but there never seemed to be any such sign. Even if such were the case,

Mama would have thought this her lot in life to bear, and it still wouldn't have stopped her from loving him or taking good care of him. Papa was always respectful of Mama in every way and shortcomings or no, he was loved by all in the community and by Mama. I've never heard my mom or anyone else speak ill of my dad. If there was anything to talk about, it was that Papa was a fun loving guy, not a churchman and only went to church on occasions to please Mama.

I vividly recall the day he died. Judith was three years old; I was six; Ionie, eight and Warren, ten. There was no funeral parlor in our community in those days, so the dead were brought back to the family home, where they laid out on an embroidered crocus bag on top of zinc and covered with ice. I was so scared by the sight of Papa lying there motionless. It was hard for my young mind to fathom my father's death.

When Mama said we couldn't go to the grave site after the funeral service, I was relieved because I didn't want to see him like that again. I didn't understand the finality that I would never see my Dad again but kept rubbing my eyes furiously to make tears come as it seemed everyone was crying. I did find out that day that I had a half-brother, my father's first child before he'd married Mama. When my brother, Sunny Boy, was introduced to us, I remember him being quite handsome, and we bonded instantly. Papa had developed cancer, but he died from cirrhosis of the liver at the age of forty-two.

On the Sunday of the funeral service, our home and yard were filled with people showing their respect, giving condolences to our family, eating, drinking, and playing religious music. Much of it was a blur except for Mama: she was leaning heavily against two women trying to help her remain upright. Then I heard three awful screams and what sounded like a chuckle from my mother. It was the unmistakable sound of deep pain that seared right down to the bone—an outcry from my mother that I will never forget. I would later come to know this as the sound of my mother crying. It was a profound display of grief from a woman who seldom showed emotion, let alone sorrow of such magnitude.

"Come Girly," the women were leading her to a chair. "You know the Lord knows best."

As I watched my mother, my heart weighed down. It frightened me to no end to see this resolute woman so vulnerable. Despite his flaws, she'd stood by Papa, caring for him through his illness without a word of complaint. Was that cry mixed with relief that Papa no longer suffered? Had she been prepared to lose her love at such a young age? Was she ready to be alone to raise four young children? His passing left a void in our lives. Her bone-chilling cry was an assault on my heart.

I understood how much Mama loved Papa and wished I had known him better. Frightened and at a loss, it pained me to know I could do nothing to help Mama in her distress but stand by and look on. That night Papa might well have been watching over us, for he was buried right in our backyard, outside the bedroom we occupied as children.

After eleven years of marriage, Mama became a widow at the young age of thirty. At six years old, unconsciously, I became my mother's keeper. Mama's heart was broken. When Papa died, I learned that you have to go on even broken-hearted. And Mama didn't skip a beat. Indeed, the following Sunday, she bundled us up and sent us off to Bible study. As before, she built up her church, which was now quite large and continued to work hard to maintain her independence and sanity. No matter how much pain she felt, her faith in God was unshakable, and she would make it through. Her church community and family embraced and surrounded her and did what they could to comfort Mama, and life simply went on. I knew things were back to normal when the neighbors, back to their nightly visits, would come knocking on the door.

"Miss Girly, mi run out of flour. Mi could borrow a little 'till you open the store tomorrow?"

Our community ran out of all sorts of things; sugar, butter, milk, eggs, or flour, and my mother would generously pony up what they needed. Of course, Mama owned the grocery store where they shopped, so if she wanted, she could have had the shopkeeper shorten their order, but that was not even a consideration. She was a community person who generously gave of all she had. Your burden was her burden, and as a woman of great character and principle, if it were in her control, she would help lift your load as though it were her own. If villagers were on their way somewhere and Mama passed them on the street, she would stop and give them a ride to their destination. We children often teased that she was the local taxi service who worked without pay.

As I grew older, I found solace in making Mama laugh even during moments of sadness. Whenever I noticed Mama was not herself, I would mimic the sound she made when Papa passed. It sounded like a laugh but she was crying. I would exaggerate my body movement and ridiculously embellish the sounds to get her attention. It was my way to lighten her mood and bring a smile to her face. It was our way of coping with loss and finding joy amidst the pain.

Chapter Four

DREAMING OF FREEDOM

*"For most of us, dreams come true only after
they do not matter, Only in childhood do we ever
have the chance of making dreams come true
when they mean everything."*

—*Unknown*

My father's passing marked the dawn of a new era for
our island nation and our family. The winds of change
were sweeping Jamaica. As the formidable Prime Minister
Bustamante declared, "A mental revolution was underway,"
heralding the promise of self-governance and newfound
independence. Visionaries like Bustamante, Norman Manley,
and Robert Lightbourne had long championed the cause of
liberation from colonial shackles, paving the way for Jamaica's
sovereignty.

The establishment of the University of the West Indies
in 1948 symbolized our commitment to education as the
cornerstone of progress. With the foundations of a two-party

political system firmly in place, Jamaica was primed to declare its independence from Britain in 1962. The air in Kingston crackled with energy as Derrick Morgan's anthem "Forward March" echoed through the streets, marking the birth of a nation and the rise of nationalism. With this whirlwind of change, my mother remained a steadfast presence in my life. Though not one to wear her emotions on her sleeve, her occasional laughter was a beacon of joy, illuminating our home with warmth and light. By the time I turned eight, Mama had become my rock, and I would do anything to bring a smile to her face and make her proud of me.

Despite the challenges of being a young widow with four children, Mama's resilience and grace shone through. Surprisingly, she found love again with Brother Francis Ford, a kind and generous soul who had long been a pillar of support for our church family. He had already donated land to build the church. They were by church standard equally yoked since they were both members of the church. Brother Ford's steadfast devotion to Mama, coupled with his gentle demeanor brought stability and joy back to our lives.

Their wedding day was a celebration of love and new beginnings. Mama, dressed in turquoise, radiated happiness. Being shorter in stature than Mama, which was gracefully overlooked by all of us, on the wedding day, Brother Ford stood on a block to be photographed as they took their vows. With, my brother, sisters, and me by her side, we stood as a testament to the strength of our family bond. Though there may have been unconventional aspects to their union, we loved him dearly and their love knew no bounds.

As Jamaica embarked on a journey of self-discovery and empowerment, so too did my mother. Mama found solace and companionship, forging a path forward with unwavering determination. With Brother Ford by her side, together they built a new home and a new life in the lush hills of Corn Piece Settlement. Though it was far from town and everyone else, they had each other.

On many more acres than our first house, this house seemed like a mansion compared to our old home. Sunbaked and verdant, the land had even more trees for us to climb and was a haven for us kids. This house had a verandah with rocking chairs to take in the cool evening breeze. Evenings would find Mama and Brother Ford on the veranda deep in conversation, a chuckle here and there speckling their chatter, or watching people go by and saying hello, or reading their bibles.

Compared to Corn Piece, Uppa Hill was more rural. As a part of the construction of our new home, the new couple built a huge grocery store, many times the size of the original one in Corn Piece where the entire village came to shop. Like Mama's father and brothers, they soon began farming, raising goats, chickens, other farm animals, and produce. Mama was busy again. We grew everything on that land; from tomatoes to callaloo, dasheen, banana, and other ground provisions, all 'organic' staples to eat off our land. During this period, before moving to our new house, my brother Daniel was born.

Amidst the hustle and bustle of everyday life, our caregivers played a pivotal role in our upbringing, filling the void left by Mama's busy days. Yet, despite her demanding commitments, Mama ensured we never missed out on the simple joys of childhood. Field trips to the zoo, lazy days at the beach, and the enchantment of watching goats being milked and collecting eggs from the chicken coop were cherished rituals in our household. As we settled into life in

Uppa Hill, a new development, we reveled in the tranquility of our surroundings, where the roads were sparse, and the sense of community palpable.

When Mama married Brother Ford in 1963, it felt like Jamaica was having a new beginning, and so were we. The sixties were a time of jubilee island wide. These goings-on of a new Jamaica, centered in Kingston, had not yet fully trickled down to 'country.' People in Hayes and Uppa Hill were more concerned with everyday life, and it wasn't an easy one. True to its promise of making life better for the underserved, the Government embarked on a housing development scheme to make housing more affordable for the poor. One of these housing schemes was in Uppa Hill Settlement. The opportunity was a defining moment for Mama. Soon more people began streaming into the Uppa Hill community, now called Corn Piece settlement, which, of course, was great news for Mama's business. Her brain, no doubt, galloping ahead to the kinds of services she could provide to her community and clients, kept her even busier than before. The more ideas she had, the more implementation she undertook. Mama's timetable was already jam-packed with farming, raising livestock, haberdashery, general goods distribution businesses, and the grocery store. But more and more people began relying on her for services which inspired new businesses.

Soon after starting the grocery store in front of our house, Mama expanded her offerings to furniture and raw materials to accommodate the community's growing needs. But even with Mama's expansion, the burgeoning settlement needed another grocery store, so one opened in our neighborhood. It turned out, however, that the proprietors had insufficient funds to keep their shelves stocked and weren't the competition Mama had expected.

"Dem no 'ave nuttin' to sell down dere," her customers soon returned, saying she was the only one who met their needs. This meant, we children, entrepreneurs in the making, had to pitch in when needed. Smaller stores kept opening to deal with the demand and as new competition increased, so did Mama's entrepreneurial drive. By then, Mama's reputation, solidly entrenched, was onto her next venture. In addition to selling groceries, clothes, and furniture, Mama now contracted with Jamaica Broiler Chicken to raise what they call machine chicken. She earned shares in the company and became a Jamaica Broiler Chicken shareholder. Mama intuitively understood how to manage risk and create multiple streams of income to no longer solely rely on the stores to provide income for the family. That Mama knew the importance of diversifying once she'd mastered a business had to be a God-given gift. But Mama wasn't the only breadwinner.

Brother Ford was gainfully employed at Monymusk estate in Lionel Town, an old sugar plantation now a distillery that made the finest Jamaican Rum. Monymusk, established in 1937, was one of the seventeen sugar factories rolled up as an important offshoot of the West Indies Sugar Co. Ltd in Frome, and the second-largest sugar factory in Jamaica. Most likely, Brother Ford had worked with the father of the singer Millie Small, of *My Boy Lollipop* fame, as he worked at the estate as a supervisor. I guess sugar was in her purview!

"Up…all you girls, get up and come help me in the kitchen." It was Mama rousing us from sleep. By ten or eleven years old, my sisters and I had to get up early to help Mama prepare a hot breakfast and pack Brother Ford's lunch, which Mama tended to herself because he was diabetic. We would prepare his special breakfast and set the table. Not one to make a fuss, the quiet Brother Ford, with his pleasant, gentle voice, never complained about what we made. So, we happily made him special dishes such as corn meal dumpling or turn corn meal, chocho (chayote) is a kind of Jamaican vegetable, cabbage, and turnip (because he couldn't eat too much starchy food). We felt sorry he had to miss out on all the wonderful breakfast foods like ackee and saltfish with dumplings, banana, plantain, and pear (what we call avocado) or mackerel rundown with yam, cassava, and dumpling.

"How is your breakfast this morning?" Mama would sit with him as he ate.

"Nice." Brother Ford would always answer. After breakfast, he'd collect his lunch, and depending on his shift that day, would ride his bike, catch public transportation, or if it were an early shift, Mama would drive him to his job. Brother Ford worked with sugar and molasses, so he'd bring home molasses to soak our sour tamarind we picked off the tree (beyond yummy when soaked), rum they never drank, and other confectionery. Every Friday, you'd find us out at the gate waiting for him to come home with goodies. My favorites: patties, banana chips, and soda.

"Thank you, Brother Ford," we'd grab our goodies and race off to a feast. He'd smile and say, "Enjoy your treat."

Under Mama's tutelage, as young girls, household helpers or not, we were versed in cleaning the house, doing laundry, cooking, and ironing our clothes. "A woman must learn how to take care of a home whether she has to or not."

Community service was ingrained in our upbringing also. Guided by the principle of "service beyond self," Mama instilled in us a deep sense of responsibility toward our community. During church fundraisers, stationed outside Moneymusk where Brother Ford worked on paydays, we eagerly joined Mama in her efforts to raise the most money We would rally the workers as they left for the day for donations and had fun doing it. Mama's generosity extended far beyond monetary contributions; she was a pillar of support for the community, providing not only essential groceries, furniture, and materials but also offering her car as a makeshift ambulance, wedding limousine, funeral hearse, and taxi service. Her unwavering dedication to bettering the lives of others, driven by an innate desire for everyone's well-being, epitomized the essence of an extraordinary woman, whose legacy of compassion and goodwill continued to inspire.

Before Alcoa polluted the air and water in the parish, Corn Piece was pristine, and the Salt River, some three miles from our home, was a community spot. With its crystal bluish-green water surrounded by the mangrove's lush foliage of old trees all gnarled and intertwined, Salt River was a respite for any burden that needed laying down. It was also the place where new converts to Christ were baptized.

Nestled amidst the verdant landscape, our home boasted proximity to the renowned hot springs, a mere three or four miles away. The mineral baths, ensconced within an ecological haven took on a mesmerizing teal hue under the scorching Jamaican sun, casting a spell of tranquility upon all who ventured there. Though the pervasive grip of poverty threatened to stifle their spirit, the resilient people of Corn

Piece somehow thrived amidst nature's bounty. Their voices, resounding with consciousness and creativity, echoed through the idyllic countryside, a testament to the enduring resilience of the human spirit.

Every Sunday morning before church, we'd go down to the river to have our weekly health bath. The Salt River was believed to have minerals with healing powers, so bathing in it was a weekly ritual for parishioners. Mostly the water was cold, but there were several thermal spots where it flowed warm. Everyone would race to get first access to the thermal spots, meaning the entire village would show up at about the same time. However, people were reasonable about sharing and yielded to newcomers though occasionally someone would want to stay longer, and we'd have to ask them to vacate since we were on a schedule.

I was always afraid to go into the water, so I would always 'quick quick' volunteer to stay home to mind the store should someone need last-minute items for their Sunday dishes. When I did go into the river, warm or not, the early morning breeze would set my teeth chattering. A point of fact, I didn't learn to swim until long after I'd come to the U.S. because I was always afraid of drowning. By the time I was in grade 7, we were always getting news that someone had drowned because of the quicksand in the Rio Minho River. I could never get that image out of my head. It may have been a carefree time for most as kids swung from nearby trees' vines and jumped into the sun-kissed water determined to splash everyone around—but it wasn't for me.

Salt River lay twenty-eight miles from the more famous hot springs at Milk River Bath, which has some of the world's most radioactive waters and because of its high levels of magnesium, sulfate, calcium, natural chloride, and a constant temperature of 95 degrees Fahrenheit, was often recommended as a healing spot, even by physicians. Meanwhile, people in Clarendon enjoyed the Salt River for many years, and though impoverished, breathing clean air, eating good organic food, and bathing in the healing rivers, they were sturdy, healthy, and happy until the government and a private sector organization got together and built around it.

Since Clarendon was the second most populous parish on the island after St. James, the government chose to develop a housing there (in the form of projects called schemes), as it would be a great place to cultivate votes! Capitalism arrived in Corn Piece in 1956, when JAMALCO AND ALCOA, the minerals mining company, began bauxite exportation. Later, in the sixties, they began commercializing the rivers of Clarendon, charging people to visit. Not long after, the Salt River, as if in defiance, dried up. It just stopped flowing! With no reason any longer to charge an entrance fee for a dried-up riverbed, the surrounding businesses shut down.

It was no surprise to the community that like a miracle, the river started flowing again after they stopped charging the entry fees. Wild but true, what was once a place of healing and baptisms disappeared when it was treated as commerce, only to be revived when set free. Today the Salt River is just as it was before the land was developed, though as of 2020, it was officially considered a tourist attraction. I hope it doesn't suffer a repeat of its earlier fate.

Chapter Five

BLISSFUL TIMES

*"I've learned that people will forget what you said,
people will forget what you did,
but people will never forget how you made them feel."*

—*Maya Angelou*

M oving from the vibrant hub of Corn Piece to the quieter Uppa Hill was a transition marked by both challenges and opportunities.

In those days, a journey to the nearest town Hayes, was a pilgrimage of sorts, undertaken for the simplest of tasks such as receiving and sending mail. Public transportation was scarce, a luxury, leaving the community at the mercy of benevolence. My mother decided to find a solution for her new community and took on the task of reshaping its access to essential services.

Mama approached the local politicians not as authorative figures but as partners in progress. Her words, sharp and precise, cut through bureaucracy and doubt alike.

"It's about more than just a post office," Mama would insist. "It's about dignity, about ensuring that every citizen, no matter their circumstance, has a fair chance to thrive."

Through tireless negotiation Mama's vision became a reality. Our humble abode was transformed into a hub of connectivity. She converted the bedroom closest to the veranda into a post office by dividing the room in half. The exterior facing window became the ideal mail pick-up spot—more ingenuity from Mama. She built a post office right in our home and became the new postmaster! People could now pick up their mail at our house. Little did I know I'd be a postwoman at such an early age! As her aids, all of us kids took turns processing, sorting, and categorizing the mail. "Now the problem is solved," Mama would say.

Uppa Hill settlement wasn't just a dot on the map; it was the very heart of our childhood, where every day brought new adventures and timeless lessons. Growing up in Jamaica was a blend of real-life tales and boundless imagination, with each moment etching itself into the fabric of our memories. Those were the happiest times of my life.

As children, we had a lot of fun in Uppa Hill. With not much entertainment, our imagination and curiosity kicked in, and we found all kinds of ways to amuse ourselves. Gem, a good seamstress, was forever making clothes for our dollies. Dressing them in different outfits would keep us busy for hours. We also had our play grocery store selling each other's goods.

"One pound of sugar and saltfish, please." Gem would order, and Judith and I would get busy scooping dirt into old, discarded tins while dried flowers stood in for saltfish.

One thing that always fascinated me was when the helper was doing laundry. She would put a big bar of blue into the water. Suddenly, a magenta-blue color would seep into the wash tub filled with white clothes! But lo and behold, the clothes would come out sparkling white. Sister Ormsby would use the rainwater collected in a drum, instead of the pipe water, to wash our hair because, she'd say, "It's soft water and much better for your hair."

I learned how to feed the chickens that would become Sunday dinner, collect their eggs for breakfast, and tend to the pigs and goats we'd soon eat. Helping to tend the animals, I learned a lot. One of my best sports was shooting birds from the sky with my catapult. Angle and trajectory served as my physics lesson. Learning how to roast them over an open pit became a lesson in gastronomic appreciation.

One of Mama's uncles, Claudy, was the butcher at the local market, and so another thing I was privy to living in the 'country' was how Sunday dinner ended up on the dinner table.

"Hold that pail steady. You understand? Don't let it go!" the butcher of the day would call to his bucket holder. Under the bucket, its crown exposed, a poor chicken would soon be headless. Fluttering about when released, it would run, reaching great distances. I was fascinated to watch a chicken with no head running fast in every direction before it finally dropped dead. The lifeless bird would then be dunked into boiling water to remove the feathers. Growing up in the country we witnessed the circle of life in action.

Far more pleasurable, and what I loved most, was riding the donkeys and horses. My grandfather, Uriah, whom we called Daddy, was a great horseman. When he visited, he rode either his horse, his donkey, or his bicycle. I loved it when he brought the horse or the donkey because he would let us take it out for a ride, and I would rush out to meet him.

"Can I ride it, Daddy? Can I?"

"You got to be careful! "

"Yes, Daddy."

Athletically inclined from an early age, I became a skilled rider. Learning to ride bareback was risky business for a young girl, but it was fun to be in command galloping on a horse or riding a braying donkey. The sense of control and freedom stayed with me forever.

There were now five children in our fold: Warren, coming of age, towering and lean, the charismatic Mr. Suave; Ionie (Gem), whose infectious laughter earned her the endearing nickname "laughing hyena" from Mama; Judith, the spirited firecracker; and completing the ensemble, my baby brother Danny and me. The antics—and *trouble*—we got into were a constant source of amusement.

On Fridays, for example, everyone went to the market to buy fresh meat. We loved going with Mama and looked forward to fresh beef soup on Saturday. Mama would call Uncle Claudy or whomever the butchers were for the weekend to be sure she got some organ meat like liver, kidney, or tripe.

It was a big deal to have freshly killed goat meat on Sunday, and it was the best when we had our first pick of the liver Uncle Claudy sold. Mama would cook the liver with fried dumplings for Saturday breakfast, which was the helper's day off. Warren, always trying to get more than his share, would snatch extra fried dumplings, hiding them in his pants pockets. Inevitably they'd leave big oily stains on his trousers.

"Warren," Mama would shout from the laundry area, and he'd know he was busted and in trouble. We'd mimic Mama's tone, but instead of calling him by his given name, we'd shout out, "'Dumpling Pocket,' Mama's calling you!" Of course, this never deterred him from pinching the fried flour because those dumplings were so good they were worth the punishment. Once, my father brought home a huge bag of flour for Warren and told him to make all the dumplings he could eat! Despite our penchant for squabbles, our bond was unbreakable. Mama's enduring connection to her own family, despite leaving home at a tender age, served as an example for us. Familial ties transcended differences and disagreements. In the Bryan household, unity and support prevailed, a testament to the profound love and solidarity that bound us together.

Sundays were marathon days. After church and dinner, Mama would pile us into the station wagon, and off we'd go to see Grandpa Uriah. On these visits, when the adults were talking 'big people business,' we had to disappear. We often played in the big tobacco house. Now and then, Mama would come looking for us. When we heard her footsteps, we'd quickly climb, like scampering monkeys, up the bamboo bars where the tobacco was put to dry. Staying perfectly still, even as the bamboo strained under our weight, we played a game to see who'd get caught first by making each other giggle. We'd watch Mama below, hollering and growing frustrated, and at just the right moment we'd jump from our perch and frighten her. Of course, this often led to a quasi-spanking.

As Grandpa got older, he spent more time with my Aunt Girty, who'd moved back home from England where she'd met and fallen in love with a fellow Jamaican, Mr. Palmer. They married and then returned home. Mama had taken care of the land their father had given Aunt Girty and she'd been sending money to build the home she would live in. Aunt Girty had two sons before she went to England, Tony and Donavan who had lived with us briefly but died at age twelve while she was away. Upon their return, she and Mr. Palmer had a son, Alister. Her return was a happy time for our family, and a goat was killed, as is customary for times of celebration. As she was grandfather's caregiver, we got to see him a lot since Aunt Girty was our favorite aunt, our favorite house to visit, and Mama's best friend. We also enjoyed Mama's other sister, Aunt Mavis's house because her kids were like us in age, and we would spend time together while the adults conversed. Aunt Mavis, however, was a schoolteacher and more of a disciplinarian while Aunt Girty was more carefree and fun. Aunt Mavis taught at Hayes Primary School where my talent as a runner became clear. Mama and my teachers knew soon enough because they could never catch me in moments of mischief.

Mama never made any significant distinction between us and the children whose parents struggled financially. In Jamaica, it is not often that people of different classes live in the same neighborhoods. In the very class-conscious country, classes didn't mix. One could simply marry their next-door neighbor and be assured they were marrying into their own class. In our neighborhood, it was different. Brother Ford had a lot of land in Uppa Hill where the Government settlement had been built. We'd built our home there and most people who lived in the settlement were not wealthy. But it was never an issue playing with other children. Mama often emphasized the intrinsic worth of every individual. And she often reminded us that God's mandate dictates that those who are blessed with abundance must extend compassion and support to those in need. For us, distinctions based on socio-economic status held no weight; in Mama's eyes, all children were equal, deserving of love, respect, and friendship.

Granted, while we most certainly could befriend the children, it was made clear they were not marriage material. Other than

44

that, our privilege didn't mean a hill of beans to Mama. Though we stood out in the community, we were simply typical children in an atypical situation. She never made it an issue, so we had lots of friends. In Mama's mind, all people were spiritually equal. Materially some just had more than others. If you were one of the lucky ones, sharing is the godly thing to do, and Mama shared.

It was both a blessing and a curse for us as children to have our prized car. We loved riding in the long station wagon, perched in the back, hatch open so we could hang our feet out, take in the fresh air, and feel the breeze tussle our hair. Sunday, however, was not one of those coveted days. Jam-packed from dawn to dusk, there was always something or other to do. We'd have preferred to chuck our Sunday routine and just be out and about with our friends, but we were expected to ride with Mama to church, and Mama would make us walk if we weren't ready on time. We soon found many ways not to be ready.

While in Mama's mind, leaving us to walk to church was punishment, for us it was liberation. If we walked we'd get to play with the other kids along the way and so we'd purposefully hide so Mama wouldn't find us either before *or* after church. Now we had playtime to, and from church!

The car, Mama's lifeline and prized possession, was rarely loaned to a single soul. Even if she wanted to, it would be difficult as she was always going somewhere. Though when she was home the car sat idle, it was only on very rare occasions that someone lucky got permission to drive it. But then, as we got older, Warren, thirteen, Gem, eleven, and I, nine, decided we wanted to learn how to drive.

"Mama," Warren would ask. "Don't you think I'm old enough to learn to drive now? Why don't you teach me?"

We would all chime in with the same question! What followed was the sucking of air through Mama's teeth and a hiss, followed by, "Go sit down somewhere."

Warren had already learned to drive from the many businesspeople and friends who visited. With no shortage of willing instructors, we younger kids also started learning how to steer the car even before our feet could touch the pedal. With Mama being uncooperative, this left us no choice but to devise a plot for opportunities to take the car out for a spin when we thought we wouldn't be busted. Scheming and planning, we were always on alert for the opportune moments.

"Look it," Warren would inform us when the time came. "Mama is sleeping."

So, it became our habit (though it was never often enough to be a habit) that we began "borrowing" the car when Mama was resting or preoccupied.

"You have the key?" Gem would ask.

"Yes. I got it."

We'd push the car out of the garage and down the road a little way from the house before starting the engine. Since we'd all watched Mama drive enough times, and had plenty of lessons from our visitors we felt confident we knew what to do. Being the middle child, I served as faithful lookout. We had signals to let each other know when it was time to return home with the "stolen" property.

Now in those days, there were no automatic cars. One had to work the gears and pedals of a stick shift. Trying not to roll back on a hill meant carefully calibrating and coordinating the foot action between the accelerator and the pedal. It was no easy task. And, as with most mischievous deeds, if you're not lucky 100% of the time, you must eventually have to pay for the crime.

And so it was that on one such escapade that Gem crashed the car! The road leading to our house was just a strip of bush that Mama had driven over again and again. There was a narrow embankment with hills on both sides. Returning home after an outing Gem took the turn from the main road too early and crashed into the embankment. Thinking we could outsmart Mama landed us in hot water. We'd overestimated our ability and underestimated the difficulties of the task at hand. Caught red-handed, no amount of denial, explanation, or escape could save us. Mama was livid, and unlike other quasi-spankings or a conk to the head, this called for serious punishment. "Save the rod and spoil the child" was her motto. Mama would whip out her contraption and whipped our behinds. The offending strap, made from strips of the car's fan belt or a braided and knotted switch was merciless on the rear end. You'd think sore tushes would have put an end to our heists, but by the time I was twelve, we all knew how to drive Mama's car!

I'd like to think underneath my mother's anger, she felt proud and impressed by her spawns' ingenuity. Though she seldom told us directly, mom was very proud of us. We were not short on ambition, thanks to her example, and we excelled in everything we did.

Singing in the church choir, for example, as a soloist, was one of my favorite things to do. "Lorna, you really have a talent for singing," Mama would say encouragingly. "Come with me and sing for the congregation." It was a special time for Mama and me. She loved taking me all over and having me sing at the different churches we visited, and I loved being with her.

During special programs for church fundraisers, I'd belt out songs like *Sweet Hour of Prayer*, and Mahalia Jackson-like, *Not My Will, But Thine Be Done* to an enthusiastic reception. It was great fun for me when the congregation would stand and cheer me on to an encore. Most satisfying was knowing that we were raising money for the church, and I was proud to be a part of something so important to Mama.

My mother's love for the church, which had caused friction within her family, did not stop Mama from trying to recruit them for God. Her sister Mavis, who had at one time given her a hard time about her involvement in the church and made fun of her devotion, became a fervent advocate. Inspired by Mama's undeniable love and commitment to her faith, it was Aunt Mavis who prompted many family members to join Mama's church after years of being inactive. One of Aunt Mavis's daughters, Opal, in fact, married a minister of the church, Winston Rowe, who officiated at both my Aunt Mavis's and my mother's funerals.

Everyone Mama met, she encouraged to join a church. She'd sometimes pick people up and give them a ride to wherever they worshipped. Hayes had three churches of different denominations blocks away from one another, all competing to build the biggest. Adamant that people needed to understand God's grace, Mama by far brought more members into her church than anyone else, but whatever church people decided to join was all right with her as long as they were worshiping.

Our household always raised the most money for our church. We grew up believing, like Mama did, that when we got to heaven, we'd receive as many stars on our crowns as we brought converts to the faith. So, as children, we were very much on the conversion path collecting our gems. And I was confident that Mama's crown would be overflowing.

Chapter Six

NEW FAMILY

"The bond that links your true family is not one of blood, but of respect and joy in each other."

—*Richard Bach*

Mama's transformation began subtly, her once lean frame now blossoming with a growing belly. Yet, amidst this change, her steadfast resilience remained unyielding. It was a scorching summer day in Jamaica when a vision in white appeared at our door, an angelic figure on a bicycle. Adorned in pristine white attire, from head to toe and carrying a black leather bag, she exuded an air of authority and grace, and commanded attention. As she swept past us with a fleeting hello and smile, I couldn't shake the feeling of intrigue stirring within me.

Entering Mama's room without being announced, the visitor's purpose was shrouded in mystery. Despite our curiosity, we knew better than to eavesdrop on adult matters. As we pressed our ears against the door, a primal scream pierced the air, not of agony, but of the miraculous act of birth: a baby! This angelic stranger had bestowed upon Mama the gift of new life, my sister Althea.

In the wake of her departure, a desire ignited within me. I yearned to emulate her, to wield the power to bring forth life as she had done. Learning that her profession was a nurse-midwife only fueled my determination. I vowed to follow in her footsteps, to become a beacon of hope and joy for families like ours. But between that transformative day and my journey through nursing school were countless trials and tribulations. Our family welcomed its newest member, a testament to the enduring bonds of love and kinship that transcend bloodlines. The memory of that day remains etched in my mind, a reminder of the extraordinary capacity for miracles amid life's tumultuous journey.

Brother Ford, calm and collected as usual, took the birth of his baby daughter, his second child, with Mama, in stride. Our large three-bedroom house seemed to get smaller with each birth. I shared a room with my brothers and two sisters. As we grew, my older brother Warren got his own room, but the rest of us bunkered down as usual. Even with a gaggle of children, nothing changed for Mama. She took it all in stride: mother, wife, businesswoman, and church founder. Because of her many businesses, she was placed in charge of the women's missionary band and the victory leaders' band for the younger congregation. Later she headed the senior citizens' group and continued spearheading the church's fundraising efforts. With the church a significant part of her life, we entertained a lot.

In America, the rotary phone had been in use since 1919, but it was not until the mid-fifties that it arrived in Jamaica and still had not made its debut in our rural corner. So it was customary for folks to just drop in unannounced. Mama a paragon of hospitality ensured our house was always warm and welcoming for unexpected guests, always fully stocked with food and drinks. Mama, a great hostess, insisted on proper behavior and etiquette. She taught us how without lecturing, and we learned by watching her actions. No matter the reason, a planned or unplanned visit, we offered guests something to eat and drink even in Mama's absence. Her attention to detail let them know they were appreciated.

Sundays after the morning church service, we'd gather for a lavish meal, often curried goat or chicken with rice and peas, and vegetables, a ritual common to the island, and shared stories. I looked forward to the dessert that awaited those who finished their plates. Even at mealtimes, Mama enforced discipline. I still recall the Sunday I faked being full to avoid eating my vegetables. Mama surprised me by telling me, "If you are too full to eat my vegetables then you are too full for ice cream. I wouldn't want your belly to burst." Lesson learned.

We all dreaded monthly Sunday wash-outs—a cleansing ritual of physics (a mixture of Epsom salts and herbs) to purge our systems of impurities. My brother Danny hated it most and would at times rather face Mama's wrath. The effectiveness of the remedy was evident when my baby sister Althea passed a large worm. For all our protests, Mama was onto something.

Power & Influence

The prevailing separation of Church and State in Jamaica and Mama's strong religious convictions prevented her from engaging in politics. However, as an influencer in the community, she often rubbed elbows with the elites and enjoyed entertaining politicians in our home no matter their political affiliation, the right-wing Jamaica Labour Party (JLP) or leftist People's National Party (PNP). There were always lively discussions of vociferous ministers one of them being our relative's in-law, Pearnel Charles, who recognized that of the fourteen parishes in Jamaica, Clarendon, was one of the most important to them. It was amazing to watch some of the most erudite men on the island quibbling as they did in the home of my mother, a high school dropout. Her social and financial prowess proved an equalizer.

Despite leaving high school before graduating herself, Mama knew the value of a good education. Not only did she make sure we were fully engaged in school, but she also wanted us to be well-rounded so she stressed extracurricular activities. It was almost unheard of in our community for people to get involved in the arts as painting or learning music. Mama, however, had an upright piano delivered to our home. She was proud and even prouder when guests would comment on it. But that piano was not just for show. We all had to take lessons. My brother Warren became a good piano player, and Mama enjoyed listening to him play while we girls sang and entertained her. She didn't laugh much, but she'd have a proud smile on her face and would give us the nod of approval when Warren rang out a 'Christian' tune. That nod was all Warren needed to 'bust a tune' on the piano from his secular repertoire which he'd taught himself. Sometimes he would accompany our in-home stage shows.

We had the most fun mimicking the worshippers at our festive church who, like at Gong Gong's (though a different denomination), you could say let it all hang out when declaring their love for God. They gave us kids plenty performance material. Our jumping up and shouting *Hallelujah* as we wildly clapped our hands, spoke in tongues, and danced, eyes closed in a trance would amuse Mama. She never encouraged us, but she certainly had a great time laughing at our antics. Sometimes Mama would laugh so hard she'd almost start crying. These were some of the only times we got to see her laugh out loud.

No matter what we got up to, Mama silently cheered us on, her eyes glistening with pride. It was wonderful, and we enjoyed her reaction as much as we enjoyed carrying on like fools. Mama was especially proud when we entertained visitors with our musical ensemble.

Despite our Christian upbringing, some of my memorable childhood times were spent under the light of the kerosene lamp, visiting the dark side in stories. Since we had no electricity and no television, we told the most frightening, duppy, or ghost stories, stories of rolling calves (mythological cows with powers), and urban myths. As the flicker of the dim oil lamp cast shadows on the walls, we enacted them in the scariest, most chilling voices. We would scare ourselves almost to death by pretending to watch ghosts pass by with their big black cats. We believed, or at least tried to convince one another, that when a big black bat flew around the house (which was common) it represented someone who'd died and come back to protect us. There was also the duppy cemetery story that went like this: when you passed a cemetery, if you pointed your finger to show someone a particular gravesite, you had to bite all ten of them because if you didn't, legend predicted they would all fall off.

It still brings a smile to my lips when I recall how we tried to out-scare each other while trying not to laugh. We used to frighten ourselves so much on the weekends that we wouldn't want to leave the room to take our evening bath. And if we didn't take our evening bath, you can bet your last dollar Mama would be around to check the bottom of our feet. A swift slap or two on our soles would have us scampering to the bathroom which, you may recall, was outside in pitch black of night!

Friday and Saturday were big nights for us kids. Children from all over the community would come by our house when their parents did their weekly grocery shopping at our store. Though we grew up in a religious household, Mama didn't stop us from understanding the secular world. We'd play together, and listen to secular music, like Byron Lee and the Dragonaires,' *Jamaican Ska,* Miriam Makeba, *Pata Pata,* and *Hound Dog* by Elvis Presley, who I was shocked to learn later was a white man. We danced the P-Juck and belted out songs. When Mama came around the corner and saw us twisting, gyrating, and shaking our booty, we would giggle and scatter.

We'd then resort to singing local nursery rhymes, having no clue at the time that some were quite scary. For example, *"I've Come to See Mary"* was about a dead girl!

"Clap hands, Clap hands
'Till Mama Comes Home
Mama bring bread for baby alone
Baby eat it off and don't give Mama none.
Mama take rock stone a lick baby down

The song was, in hindsight, abusive! I loved our folk songs too, *Linstead Market; Long Time Gal Mi Never See You, and Brown Girl in the Ring.*

We would dance to those songs, flipping our skirts this way and that. The slave negro spirituals passed down from our ancestors during slavery, such as *Sammy Dead*, about an overworked dead slave, *Hill and Gully Rider*, an escaped slave, and *Chi Chi Bud Oh*, the call and response song of slaves as they toiled in the hot sun were also island favorites. And how could I forget Harry Belafonte's Calypso *Banana Boat*:

Day O,

Daylight come

And we want go home.

We played traditional games such as hide and seek, jacks, gigs, marbles, baseball, volleyball, jump rope, and hopscotch. We were never bored, at least not that I can remember. Later in the evening hours, we took over the big hallway of the house and played around doing 'dirty dancing' style moves and making fun of each other.

Christmas, however, is my favorite memory of my time in Jamaica. It was magical, and the rituals indelible. Because Mama had cultivated strong relationships in the community, each Christmas season, when it was time to paint the house a different color for the holidays, as was customary, there was no shortage of help. Like many Jamaican households' holidays were a time of camaraderie and renewal. There were seasonal drapes to hang, bed linens to change, silver to polish, and the 'good' dishes that sat in cabinets all year to be washed. Finally, there was the thorough house cleaning in preparation for the festivities and the visitors who'd drop by with holiday cheers and for a drink. This was when Brother Ford's rum and other

Moneymusk goodies he brought home came in handy. Then there was cake topped with icing to bake, punch, sorrel, ginger beer to be made, and a spread to be cooked, so food was always available. Lined up in the glass cabinet were beautifully decorated fruit and rum cakes with icing and glistening silver balls every day from December 25th to New Year's Eve.

So, at Christmas time, our white house with its red roof would take on a new color, and the tree trunks would be whitewashed. The men in the community all came together to help spruce up the house inside and out. Mama fed them from big pots of food she'd prepared and gave them a Jamaican man's coveted libation: Rum, Red Stripe, and Guinness stout. Being a staunch Christian did not stop Mama from bringing in the Christmas spirit.

Though she never drank in front of anyone, she'd cheer on the crew clinking their glasses of libation. When the work was done, Mama handed out produce and other groceries for the men to take home to their families. If the jobs were big ones, in addition to goods and produce, she'd show her appreciation by saying, "Have a Merry Christmas, and may God bless you and your family, "and hand the worker's money along with a chicken and a loaf of Jamaican hard-dough bread.

"Thank you, Sister Ford, and Merry Christmas." They'd chime.

There is absolutely nothing better in the world than some fresh, hot harddough bread spread with butter. It truly, for me, was a magical Christmas in Uppa Hill, different from the commercial Christmases I would experience in the United States. At home, it was all about giving thanks for our blessings and welcoming guests who'd drop by for the requisite black cake with icing and a Christmas drink. Whatever Mama could do to help those in need, a giving Christmas was always a part of our ritual. When customers, more like a close-knit family, could not afford items from our store, Christmas or not, Mama would either put their groceries on credit, or "trus" as it's called in Jamaica or offer them the opportunity to work in exchange for the goods. Growing up in Jamaica was a beautiful time for me.

Chapter Seven

THE CARDINAL RULES

"Patience and perseverance have a magical effect before which difficulties disappear, and obstacles vanish."

—*John Quincy Adams*

As in all families, with good memories comes challenging times. But whatever was happening in our family, we did our best to be there for each other. My sobering moment came when I was about ten years old and true to word, my family rallied.

At nine or ten years old, things go from carefree to serious business for some kids in Jamaica, and my blissful life came to a screeching halt. I'd graduated from Hayes primary and gone on to May Pen Junior secondary, joining my older sister Gem two years ahead of me. I felt all grown up. It was exciting to attend school outside of my district and to take public transportation like the other children. Now and then, Mama would drive us, but I preferred the camaraderie on the bus. Just as business was innate to my mother, my superpower at May Pen Junior

Secondary was my athletic abilities. I must have gotten the least spanking out of all the children there because I was fast on my feet from a very young age.

I became a bona fide athlete at May Pen, winning every prize in sports, be it track and field, long jump, high jump, and netball, you name it. Then, however, it was time to move on to high school. In order to go from junior high to high school, all students must take what is known as the common entrance exam. To get into the high school of one's choice, one had to pass the exam. The higher the cumulative marks, the greater the chance of getting into a top school. What was normal then, but seems cruel and usual punishment now, much like corporal punishment, is that the names of the kids who passed the exam were printed in the national newspaper. Worse was the emotional hardship and embarrassment of those who had failed as their names, of course, were not inked.

When I was about ten years old, I took the confounded exam and did not pass. I was devastated and, needless to say, came home crying. Of course, my incredible Mama already knew as my name wasn't in the paper, and she was ready with words of comfort and encouragement when I got home. Instead of being angry, Mama sat me down and said, "Lorna, the Lord has this in his hands. There must be a reason you didn't pass. Believe me, all will be okay because He has another plan for you. All you have to do is work harder next time, and you will be fine."

Well, that helped, but I was still upset, not to mention the embarrassment. To Mama, the eternal optimist and believer, all failings meant something better was coming along, for my good. As it turned out, Jamaican schools were transitioning from the forms system to the grades system. Because I was in-between grade age, I never had to take the exam again. The school's solution was to create a special transitional grade six for those whose birthdays fell outside the eligible months for regular admission. Our sixth-grade class was wonderful, and I loved my classmates. Before going off to our respective secondary high schools, the year we spent together was memorable and empowering! Once again, Mama had been right. I became a standout athlete for three years at May Pen Junior Secondary, proudly accepting the title of Champion Girl—a title only given to girls with the highest sports achievement. May Pen Junior Secondary, as it turned out, was a feeder for Vere Technical High School, one of the most renowned schools on the island for sports. Because I had not passed the common entrance exam, God's plan, Mama said, was for me to go to this particular school where my talent could shine. I recovered from failure, and my confidence soared. Shortly after, I passed the grade nine achievement test and landed at Vere Technical High School.

Founded in 1964, by the time I got to Vere Technical High its reputation and prowess in athletics were well known. It was purported to be the breeding ground of Olympic Champions. It had won the most Girl Championships on the island and continued its domination in track and field through 1993. Maintaining a stranglehold on the trophy to its rival, the boy's team at Kingston College, Vere turned out Olympic legends such as Merlene Ottey, who led the Vere takeover in 1979.

I truly believe that had I stayed in Jamaica, I would've had the opportunity to compete in the Olympics. Indeed, the recognition of Jamaican sprinting dominance in the Olympics is an honor that belongs almost exclusively to Clarendon with the exception, of course, of the incomparable Usain Bolt from

Trelawny. And, I still have athletic arms to show for my years of solid training, ha-ha!

We were growing up, and it was time to indoctrinate us in the cardinal rules of life lest we forget. The trifecta: God, education, and perseverance were the basis of Mama's child-rearing. She had many mantras, proverbs, adages, and rules to live by. *Rule Number One: Fear God, but know he is a loving God.* Mama believed when people did bad things, they would suffer God's vengeance, and it was not man's job to cause any suffering. Likewise, she pointed out that although good things may happen to bad people and bad things happen to good people, in the end, what looks bad could be a blessing, and what looks like a good may not be. As Mama said, it was all in our perspective because God is always present, and He will present Himself right on time for the right reason. So leave it up to God.

Not everyone in our community was a churchgoer, let alone Christian. Some believed in 'witchcraft and folk magic,' a religion called Obeah. The colonialists outlawed it in the 1800s. Obeah, a dynamic religion, had its origins in Africa from the Akan Ashanti, Coromatins, and other tribes who made up the majority of slaves in Jamaica. All over the Caribbean and Latin America, where the enslaved were brought and sold, you'll find similar oppression of African-origin religions—Vodou in Haiti, Santeria in Latin colonies such as Cuba, Condombé in Brazil, and so on. Of course, Obeah was no more nefarious than Christianity, but the white colonialists, wanting to prevent the Africans from communicating, insisted it should be banned.

Since Jamaicans have a way of ignoring authority, they ignored the colonists. To this day, Pukkumina and Obeah are very much alive and well on the island, and Jamaica remains an island of folklore, magic, and spirituality. Many revivalist churches incorporated old African and new European customs. However, Mama always told us that she believed Obeah was nonsense. Her God was the Almighty, and no matter what other people said, we should believe and trust only in Him.

That she was a very young woman with four children when my biological father died was proof enough for her, for she was only comforted by the knowledge that it was God's plan. A loving God, she believed, had relieved the pain and suffering her husband had endured, and helped her through her silent anguish from his drinking. As a Christian, my mother didn't believe in divorce. She would not have left him 'till death did they part. Had he not died, she'd have lived a long life of suffering and simply made the best of it. After Papa died, God sent her a husband of equal yoke, a man of God, her Brother Ford. So, God has a reason for everything that happens.

Rule Number Two: There is no need to fight with words or fists because God is your sword. Mama was opposed to any form of arguing or revenge. She left all her battles up to God, who'd fight them for her in His way. The irony was everybody in our community was afraid of or intimidated by the ball of fire called Mama. To this day, I hate arguing and fussing because I saw for myself that one did not have to engage in battle to command respect.

Often people's backs would straighten or they would leave when they saw Mama coming. She never took it as a sign they didn't like her, and thought it funny when we told her that people would purposely turn and walk the other way when they heard her car engine. They all knew she ran a tight ship at home and that she was no joke. She had never consciously done, nor would she ever do anything to hurt or frighten anyone. Yet, though she spoke softly, she carried a big stick, a big presence—and the love of God in her heart. Without a battle of words, Mama earned the respect of the community through her actions.

Rule Number Three (and OMG this was a biggie): Don't disgrace the family. As kids, we felt the pressure of doing nothing 'out of order.' We had to be impeccable at all times and carry ourselves with dignity and deference. Decorum was the word. I believe that though successful, Mama over-compensated partly because she'd dropped out of school and decorum certainly figured into that. Her lack of formal education shaped her in ways that even she didn't understand. Force though she was, she strived to keep a certain image.

In terms of business, Mama was the most financially successful in her family. Always open to change—forever learning new things, she would say learning was essential for growth. One of her favorite scriptures to repeat to us was, 2 Timothy 2:15, "Study to show thyself approved unto God, a workman that needed not be ashamed." Her work ethic was embodied in the quote by Eric Hoffer. "In a time of change, the learner will inherit the earth; while the learned find themselves beautifully equipped to deal with a world that no longer exists." As much as Mama had learned, she still struggled with not graduating, though you couldn't outwardly tell.

Mama was strict with her appearance and expected this of us. She never straightened her hair or wore a wig. She preferred it natural, neatly tucked in a net under a hat or a scarf tied tightly beneath her chin. She was known for her beautifully colored scarves and felt naked if she left the house without her head covered. A hat was required at church while worshiping, so Mama believed in wearing one whenever outside our home.

We always saw Mama as very regal. She took great pride in her conservative appearance. I still have a few of her scarves, which I kept after she passed, and occasionally, I use them to wrap my hair at night to sleep. It feels comforting.

Rules Number Four and Five: Waste not. What's of no value to one could always benefit someone else. And Pride is no virtue.

There was also the issue of our shoes. Mama didn't like store-bought shoes because the roads in the area we lived in were terrible, and they wouldn't last long before looking raggedy and torn-up. Our special shoes were made by the shoemaker, and sadly for us kids, seemed to last many lifetimes. The longer they lasted, the less often we got new ones. Sometimes we'd soak them in water or walk-through puddles and twist them up in the hopes of hastening the purchase of a new pair. At best, they were unfashionable; at worst, downright ugly, and very unlike the fashionable Bata brand shoes that were around at that time.

One Christmas, Mama bought me a pair of really cute "regular" shoes. It turned out they were way too small for my feet. I didn't say anything because I really liked them, so I tried my best to make them work. They were so tight that they gave me blisters, and unlike the hand-me-down clothes, I couldn't even give them to my younger sister because I had the smallest feet in the family. When Mama found out about the blisters, she took the shoes away. She felt awful that I'd suffered and told me I should never hide something like that again. Pride was not a virtue. Not too long after, I saw someone at our church wearing my shoes. Waste not.

Growing up in the church meant we adhered to strict mores and dress codes. My Aunt SaVie, a great seamstress, made all our clothes according to Mama's instructions. Most of the time, the raw materials Mama gave Aunt SaVie, and the styles she requested were blah. Aunt SaVie's daughters, meanwhile, did not believe in church rules, so they wore fashionable clothes like the ones Gem used to make for our dolls. Older than us, whenever they gave us clothes made originally for them that they didn't want, Mama allowed us to accept them, though she would never have bought them herself.

While the hems on our normal dresses had to be below our knees, these new dresses were above! Mama would instruct us to let out the hems, but our cousins, forever coming to our aid, would tell Mama to stop dressing us like old people. She would grumble, but she mostly turned a blind eye even as some church members complained. Mama would allow some flexibility, though she had her limits.

As I write this, I'm all smiles thinking back on some of our daring escapades. On most occasions, Mama would shake her head and smile, which made me appreciate her wisdom. They were just things that came with the rites of passage. Others, however, were downright dangerous.

While we did have beautiful hair as kids, it was the oddest reddish color and we were teased because of it. When we tried to change its color, it was a standout catastrophe. We'd learned how to use black shoe polish mixed with kerosene oil to make our hair black and shiny. We hadn't considered what would happen when it touched any material, God forbid a flame. Imagine what Mama thought when she came into our room one morning only to find our pillows and bed linens covered in a greasy black substance smelling like kerosene. She couldn't understand why in God's heaven we would do something like that. It was another fan belt switch moment. Teenage girlhood was turning out to be a time when our creativity landed us in such serious hot water.

Then there was the hot comb incident. My cousins were a lot of fun, and we learned worldly things from them. They taught us about using fruit punch to make our lips red since we weren't allowed to wear lipstick, and how to straighten our hair with a hot-pressing comb. This was a no-no for Mama.

Gem, of course, came up with a creative way to straighten our hair using a dinner fork. We'd put the fork on the flaming stove until it was very hot, then pull it through our hair! Can you imagine? Once again, we waited until we thought Mother was asleep. What we hadn't planned on was that she could smell our hair burning. Busted, we ran away when she came into the kitchen. We didn't get far and Mama showed up when we were in bed to give us a spanking.

This was almost as big as the car episode, maybe bigger in Mama's mind, because she believed we could have burned down the house. We needed the grace of God and maybe our Stepdad to save us. But even Brother Ford, our go-to person for hideout spots and protection couldn't save us. She could not understand why we'd taken such a risk for the sake of our vanity. No amount of pleading could save us, and the end of this saga was not a pretty one for any of us.

If there was ever a time I heard Mama and Brother Ford disagree, it was about her punishments, especially when she got us in bed. Whenever she checked the bottoms of our feet after our nightly bath, if they weren't clean, let's just say there was no snoozing for a while after we were caught. We could hear Brother Ford, scolding her from their room. "Sister Ford, what did I tell you about waking up the kids to beat them after they go to bed? You have to stop that. It's not good for them."

"But these kids are 'hard of hearing.' As the saying goes, 'hard heads make for soft behinds.'" As mom would caution,

"If you give them an inch, they will take a mile!" And as often as Brother Ford would try to save us, we all knew Mama was undeniably in charge. Her mantra, "I don't want any lazy children in my house," emphasized her belief that cleanliness is next to godliness. Of course, our stubbornness was a trait we undoubtedly inherited from her. Still, it didn't matter what we did as children; we just could not outsmart Mama.

Rule Numbers 6 7 8, 9: Don't do the crime if you can't do the time. Don't let ego get in the way of making a life for yourself, and don't expect anything to be handed to you, times two. There is a reward in figuring things out as you go along. Her saying, "Work never killed anyone, but being lazy will," stuck true in my later years. Mama's creed is that God will take care of the rest if you work hard and do the right things in life.

Growing up, we girls learned to run the house, while the boys worked every day with Mama, from spending hours in the grocery store to tending to the land and livestock. "There is value in hard work, but i*dle time is the devil's playground.*" If Mama happened to pass by and one of us was doing nothing, she'd say, "Go get a book. Do something before something do you." We didn't like it at the time, but she was right, and we were the better for it.

Rule Number 10: "Always give to your community." Whether it was raising money for the church, giving a ride to someone on the street, or feeding a hungry child, my mother knew the true value of supporting her community and expected nothing in return. She even took children in need into our home, always believing goodness is passed on and paid forward. Be grateful for everything, no matter how small.

As we got older and spent time with Mama either in the U.S. or Jamaica, she always wanted us to give her whatever we could to take back to Jamaica, not for herself but for others. She felt our lives in the U.S. were full of bounty, and, in her mind, there would be no imposition for us to give away some of our many possessions, no matter the cost. Often, Mama took home clothes, perfumes, household items, toys—anything she felt would make life better for others. She reasoned that these things would be of greater value to the people of Jamaica. When she got home, she would proudly share the gifts, all the while showing off her children's philanthropic commitment. Even when we bought gifts for our family and friends at home, Mama wanted to be the one to give them on our behalf since she knew who needed them most.

I'll never forget the first time I saw Mama go into a Kentucky Fried Chicken restaurant in Jamaica and convince the manager to give her all the leftover food for the seniors at her church. Growing up, Mama indeed showed us that, *It takes a village to raise a child and that* giving and making people's lives better was the ultimate gratitude to God for all he had given us.

Long before this African saying was attributed to Hillary Clinton, we were well acquainted with *Rule Number 11: It Takes a Village.* Word of our misbehaving would get to Mama even before we got home from school. When Mama got news from the 'chatty-chatty' neighbors, she would pick us up from school. And when we saw her coming, we knew we were in for it. Under the guise of tickling us, she'd pinch us in a loving but reprimanding way. Held hostage in her car, we couldn't run away and she kept at it the entire ride home. When we threatened to jump out of the moving vehicle, she'd call our bluff and dared us to do it. "Jump, go ahead and jump," she'd say. All this while she expertly drove the car down the rocky, uneven dirt roads. It was quite a scene as we attempted to stay beyond her reach while desperately trying to hold on and not get knocked about as the car drove into ditches and over rocks. There was no backing down until we were sufficiently punished. Mama was not about to spoil us. And she chose the rod of punishment according to the crime: a conk on the forehead, a switch to the leg, not allowing us to go play with our friends, or the almighty strap, which was always conveniently located in her bra for easy access. She didn't use it often but had her ways to make sure we obeyed and followed expected daily routines.

There were times we thought we could outrun Mama and believe me, I was born to run and I was fast. At school, I was safe, but relying on quick feet didn't save me or any of us one bit because Mama had time on her side. She would let us run and we hoped that she'd get tired and forget about the punishment. But when we least expected it, she'd get the best of us.

"You will thank me later for these spankings. Believe me." Mama always said. It's good discipline for your future."

I think harsh spankings should be banned. Caring parents spank their children not to abuse them but rather to set necessary limits. One mistake could alter a life irreversibly. While there are better disciplinary tools today than corporal punishment, children need clear boundaries, and a lack of accountability and necessary discipline fails them. Fear is a great motivator. No one wants to watch their child put their hand in the flame without intervening. Nor did anyone want a thrashing—certainly not from Mama. Never vicious or ill-intended, Mama's spankings were consequences of our actions: *Don't do the act unless you can pay the consequences.* I can think of many an incident that could have derailed our lives had we not feared Mama's strap.

Even as we got older and grew taller, Mama always made it clear we were never too big for her to administer a punishment.

One day I did something wrong and was due for a whipping. I thought I was grown up so I challenged and stood up to Mama as if to say, "Go ahead, hit me." Unfazed, she delivered what I thought was my final thrashing as a teenager. In a moment of insolence, I asked if she had finished and earned myself a second whipping. That was the last one I can remember, but I'd finally learned my lesson. Mama always wins.

Occasionally, for some misdeed while working with Mama in the grocery store my brother also needed a visit from the strap. At the end of the day when no one was in the store, the race would begin. Mother would lock the door with Warren inside. He would try to hide and outrun her by zipping up and down the aisles and zigzagging over the counter. He would run like crazy dodging Mama as she relentlessly chased him, strap held high. He'd be giggling as he'd escape her by inches. My sisters and I would stand near the door, and when my big brother got close, we'd open the door for him to escape. It was a ridiculous scene, and we always got what was coming to us, but we made it fun all the same.

Though strict when we were young, Mama truly enjoyed the energy of youngsters and loved having us around. She also loved animals, which we had aplenty. We had dogs, even toy ones, and just about any toy animal that moved. Her favorite was the bobbleheads, which seemed like the strangest thing to us, but she loved having them in the car, watching them wiggle and make noises as she drove. In her later years, I brought her many mechanical gifts because her fondness for them seemed to grow right along with her age. I remembered one Christmas she spent with me in Beverly Hills. I got these special colorful Christmas reindeer decorations with moving heads. She was tickled pink and thoroughly enjoyed them.

Rule Number 12: Anything you want in this life, you can achieve it. The sky was not the limit. For her, there was no limit. When we'd accomplished anything major, Mama only smiled and said, "That's good." However, as we traveled the community, everyone would stop to congratulate us and tell us how proud our mom was of us. Apparently, Mama couldn't stop talking about our successes and enjoyed bragging about her children. She made us feel we could achieve anything and wanted success for us. We were *her* children, which meant we were to stand on our own two feet, make a life for ourselves, and excel at whatever we did. Mama wholeheartedly believed that because we were more fortunate than other kids, we had to become more than what was expected of others.

Rule Number 13: To whom much is given, much is expected; follow your heart's desire and go for it."

Unlike many well-to-do Jamaican parents—the aspirational ones who live vicariously through their offspring I don't remember Mama telling us, trying to persuade, or hardwiring us into a career choice. Unlike those who wanted their children to graduate as lawyers or doctors from Ivy League schools to boot we were free to follow our passions. I do remember her always asking what we wanted to be when we grew up but never tried to force us in any one direction except to give us access to the best education. Mama had long set her sights on her children becoming educated and was forever pointing out the habits of successful people. There was no shortage of talk about successful people in our home. Subliminally, she was planting success in our heads. Yes, she wanted us to follow our bliss as long as the other side of that blissful door was a success.

As kids, there was a game we played. It goes like this: someone asks, "Who am I?" You can be a rich man, poor man, beggar or thief, lawyer, doctor, Indian, or chief. As you mention each one of the characters, you point to each person in the circle. None of us wanted to be the poor man, beggar man, or thief. This game reinforced what we already knew: we had to make a good life for ourselves.

Thanks to Mama's diligent efforts in sending us to America, each of us found success in various fields, surpassing what she envisioned for us in Jamaica. The wealth and opportunities afforded by America far outweighed any prospects of returning to Jamaica. We were instilled with a strong work ethic from a young age, emphasizing action over mere words. At times, I wondered whether Mama's reluctance to inquire about our aspirations stemmed from her hope that we would eventually take the reins of her empire, ensuring its generational succession and expansion beyond her own vision. However, none of us followed that path. Instead, we playfully teased her, acknowledging that her exceptional guidance had propelled each of us to exceed expectations individually, thereby becoming the true legacy of her remarkable achievements.

Rule Number 14: Effort In equals Results Out—everything carries a price tag, whether for good or ill. Thanks to Mama, I now face challenges with unwavering confidence, viewing obstacles as steppingstones to greater heights. Her indomitable spirit inspired me not to rest on my laurels after becoming a nurse-midwife. Instead, I followed her entrepreneurial footsteps, leveraging her teachings to grow my business and extend my impact. Like her, I surrounded myself with successful individuals, embraced hard work, prioritized continuous learning, and dedicated myself to serving my community. Mama's message of living selflessly and purposefully resonated deeply within me, guided my actions and shaped my life's foundation as I ventured into the world.

Chapter Eight

THE VALUE OF CHANGE

The key to all life is value.
Value is not what you get,
It's what you give.

—*Jay Abraham*

In Jamaica, children graduate from primary education (high school) at age fifteen or sixteen and are considered adults. There are a few choices. Go to university, continue on to A-Levels—two additional years of advanced high school courses, get a job, go to a training school to learn a skill like typing, or start setting your sights on marriage. If not married, they'll likely live in the family home until one of the above happens. Most middle-class families simply expand the family compound to accommodate their children while the more disadvantaged families live together in the same house with their parents and grandparents. Generally speaking, unmarried children never leave home unless they further their education abroad or at The University of the West Indies.

Many children of able parents were sent away to school in England, Canada, or the United States. Many of those left behind were idle with too much time on their hands, thus easy picking for the devil's workshop. Young people, girls, way too often found themselves pregnant. Mama, always concerned about her girls was a vigilant gatekeeper and the boys in the community knew to steer clear.

Unknown to us, while other children in the neighborhood were starting families, Mama was fast-tracking our departure. She certainly didn't want to sully the family name with one of us getting pregnant out of wedlock, and the added burden of Jamaica's budding political challenges could make things worse.

It was either shortly before or after Michael Manley came to power that our family began leaving the island. Though Mama had no political affiliation, she admired the benevolent and strong-willed politician for looking out for the poor. Begging was something Mama abhorred, and she never wanted to see anyone having to beg to live. His ideology of raising up the impoverished sat well with her. Long before democratic socialism, Mama had set up her system of caring for the poor. She created daily tasks to employ and empower them, from helping them start businesses, to finding them work in the yard, washing dishes, feeding the pigs, or cutting the grass. She would do whatever she could to ease their burden. But not everyone in the country felt like she did. And things were getting worse for the poor as political warmongering devastated the island.

Ten years after Independence, Jamaica, instead of moving forward, was sliding backward. Trickle-down greed, and increasing power grabs between parties, had significant consequences for its citizens and the economy. As the son of one of Jamaica's elite families, Michael Manley had resisted political entanglement for years to avoid criticism of currying favor. But in 1972, the devastatingly good-looking politician became the fourth Prime minister of the island and proved himself to be a dynamic and popular leader who had a warm relationship with the country's poor. Setting his sights on domestic reform politically and socially, he radically upended Britain's imperialist hold on the island. Manley changed everything—from the style of dress to free schooling for the masses to ideas of mastery and servitude to land redistribution and democratic equality. For the first time since independence, a leader broke with the stifling imposition of the island's elite, calling for a replacement of the constitutional monarchy. He envisioned a Jamaica that represented all its people.

His 'radical' ideology, diplomatic friendship with more hardline leftist leaders such as Fidel Castro of Cuba, and his support of Angola that'd staved off apartheid, was of concern. It was enough to scare the U.S. government and the rich folks on the island whose wealth depended on trade with the U.S. Critical of Manley's Democratic Socialist political philosophy, relations between the United States and Jamaica worsened. Failed talks between U.S. National Security Advisor Henry Kissinger, Vice President Spiro Agnew, and Michael Manley, fueled propaganda that U.S. was attempting to destabilize the Jamaican government. There were even accusations that the CIA was supplying weapons to the right-wing opposition party, JLP. The question of destabilization was never resolved.

Dismantling poverty, Manley would learn, would not to be easy. Under his leadership, Jamaica experienced a significant escalation in political violence, and his ideology led to capital flight as masses of wealthy Jamaicans fled the island with their cash and other assets, further devastating the economy.

Even though the times would prove challenging for Jamaicans, the country's unrest was not the reason any of us left the island. A few years before Manley came to power Gem, my jovial sister who was always laughing and happy, left Jamaica a sad girl. Gem, you see, was being pursued by her gentleman friend. Totally in love, she reciprocated his affections, sneaking him into the house many a night when Mama was in bed. Unluckily, Gem got caught, which earned her a one-way ticket to New York to live with our grandaunt. I've always believed Gem's first love was her soulmate and for most of her young life, she never stopped loving him. Mama, however, was not having her children sidelined by love.

A year or so later, my six-foot-four, good-looking brother, Warren, left his broken-hearted suiters for Canada. Warren was not smitten with any of them, but the girls wouldn't leave him alone, often inveigling him to sneak out with them at night to the deserted train line. Mama wasn't having it.

It would've been my turn to leave next in terms of age, and I was looking forward to it after graduation. Only something happened. Trouble always found the independent Judith, and so Mama decided to send her away before me. It took one letter from a boy for her to reverse that plan. It all started at the postal agency in our home. I was a teenager when I received a letter from a boy in a neighboring town. He was a good church member from another district, and we'd met during a church outing. It was now the seventies, and Uppa Hill still didn't have telephones. I'm sure the boy, out of respect, preferred not to show up at our door unannounced and so he wrote me a letter. Mama, the postmistress, of course, intercepted the letter and within minutes after reading it she got in her car, drove to the other town to find out who this boy was, and forced his parents to have him end all communications with me.

Shortly after, having not yet graduated high school, I was sent to Canada. Mama said it was because she wanted all of her children to get an education and make lives for themselves before getting married and having babies. But as she well knew, love had its own agenda, and that scared her. By then, Mama felt she'd given me enough of a foundation to manage abroad and trusted I would not fail, but make her proud. I was packed off to finish high school in Toronto where my brother Warren had migrated years before.

Once a British colony, Canada remained a constitutional monarchy until 1982. It was far easier to get a passport to another Commonwealth country than to America during these times of unrest. No other family in our community could afford to send their children away for school during those days. Those who did manage to go to the U.S., Canada, and the Bahamas were mainly migrant workers for farming or domestic work. In a way, I was excited when it was my turn to leave for Canada. Though I was doing well in track and field at Vere Technical High School, going to Canada trumped athletics.

It was both happy and sad to say goodbye to my childhood friends, my younger siblings, Judith, Daniel, Althea, Mama, and Brother Ford, but this was a rite of passage. There were many tears of both joy and sorrow when I left. Sad as I was to leave, I was excited about the idea of traveling to a foreign country. I vowed to keep in touch through letters and looked forward to seeing them when I returned on vacation. And so I boarded my first airplane flight to Canada.

The Great White North, so called because it's the second-largest country in the world, to me was another world. Far from Corn Piece, Mobay, Ocho Rios, or even Kingston, Toronto was a cosmopolitan, modern city. Unlike its name, white north, Toronto is a diverse city with big skyscrapers and smooth black tarred roads. Canada's multiculturalism was as impressive as Jamaica's. Fifty percent of the residents belong to a minority population group, and Toronto is known as the most multicultural city in the world behind London.

Eglington and Bathhurst, known as Little Jamaica, was an ethnic enclave with a large Caribbean population. My brother and cousins lived in the Pape and Danforth area. My disappointment was immediate when I arrived at my brother's house. It amounted to a boarding house for the gazillion relatives he'd sponsored from Jamaica. They all seem to live with him! Far less comfortable than our spacious home, my living situation left a lot to be desired, and it would take some getting used to. I therefore spent a lot of time at the home of my cousin Netty and her husband Oliver. It wasn't hard to find a Church of God of Prophecy in the neighborhood and Pastor Hubert Martin, the minister of the church I attended, turned out to be an old family friend. I would later live with him and his wife, Bonnie, and their young son Ian, who I now consider my little brother. It was a more amenable and conducive arrangement than living with my brother. This pleased Mama a great deal. From the moment I landed, Gem, became Mama's watchful eye across water. Gem and I were very close as children, sharing the same birthday and got even closer as adults. Though we lived in different countries, she made sure I had everything I needed.

Every so often, a care package would arrive with money and other goodies. "I just sent you a care package. What else do you need? How are things going over there? How is Warren?" She'd ask on our frequent calls.

As my de facto parent, Gem reported to Mama how I was adjusting. She wasn't much older than me, but like Mama, she was firm in her opinions about my future and took on Mama's role of ensuring I stayed on the right track. The transition to high school in Canada after completing only a year in Jamaica proved to be a challenge. The discrepancy in grade levels between the two school systems meant I had a lot of catching up to do academically. Moreover, adapting to a new culture presented its own set of hurdles. Despite Canada's multicultural ethos, those who were different often became targets of ridicule. My accent became a source of amusement for my peers; they would mock me when I pronounced words "improperly." For instance, I would add 'H's to words like "Oven" and omit them from words like "Her," "He," or "Him." To this day, I occasionally catch myself slipping into these speech patterns. While I understood the correct pronunciation, the environment I grew up in often prevailed.

Had I stayed in Jamaica, I would've graduated high school at sixteen, or age eighteen if I'd gone on to A 'Levels. At Wellesley High, the private school I attended in Toronto, I had to do the work of three different grades simultaneously to catch up. By graduation at age eighteen, I was still short one subject. Keeping up with the workload, with barely passing grades, I was too ashamed to tell my sister I was one subject short of graduating. When Gem began making plans for me to attend university, I told her I wanted to work for a year before college.

"Whaaat! You can't do that, Lorna!" She let out a scream worthy of the news that someone had died. "What do you expect me to tell Mama? Plus, if you go out and start working and making money, you may never go back to school." Gem cried for a long time on the phone. When we signed off, she reminded me again how important my education was to my future and my family. In my mind, I only needed one science credit, and I knew what I had to do. It was no big deal. I'm not sure why I wasn't upfront with her; maybe I was ashamed, but I am my mother's child, determined and striving. I knew without a single doubt that I would complete my course, so I couldn't appreciate why she was so worried.

I decided to go to summer school but enrolled in a public school this time instead of going back to a private school. As it turns out, and as my mother would have predicted, something good comes from every disappointment.

I'd experienced prejudice with my guidance counselor. She'd made me feel I wasn't smart enough to go to nursing school and recommended I become an X-ray or lab technician—jobs for lower-skilled people, no doubt because of the color of my skin. I was short one subject I could easily have picked up in summer school but she never suggested it. Not a single concern did this woman have about my recent transition and why I was short a subject. As a brainwashed victim, she'd ascribed all her prejudices to my skin color and didn't even think I could have been raised more privileged than she could ever be. In her eyes, I was less than but like Mama would say, her concern was no concern of mine.

In Jamaica, where 92.1 percent of the population is Black, though classism surely felt like oppression and cut along color lines, there was never a question of my ability to succeed. Black people were lawyers, doctors, judges, classical pianists, engineers, Indian chiefs, physicists, you name it. As long as you had the aptitude, you could be whatever you wanted—at least to a certain degree, especially if you had the right connections and financial resources. Now I was in a school with only two other Black students at the time, one being my cousin, (Myrna Bryan) and faced with prejudice that might otherwise have eroded my self-confidence. Instead, it brought out the warrior in me. After all, I'm Clarendonian, from the parish of *Tallawah*.

In the public school, my teacher was encouraging, understanding, and extremely helpful. The guidance counselor showed me how to select the right classes as prerequisites for nursing school, which I took in addition to my missing class. She even helped me apply for the nursing program. While finishing my prerequisites, I worked at the local hospital in the nutrition department, delivering and clearing patients' food trays. It wasn't a glamorous job, but it was a stepping-stone to my future. I got to learn about hospitals and how to interact with patients. In a way, I was just like Mama when she started out by selling coal—there was a need, and my ego never got in the way. It also reinforced that working with patients was my passion. I learned a lot and got paid.

That summer, not only did I complete the one chemistry class I needed, but I also took an extra physics and calculus class and passed them both with flying colors, A-grades. The following year, I made it into the nursing program of my choice, and Gem was ecstatic. In addition to Gem's care packages, Mama sent money from Jamaica to make sure I had what I needed. It was all opposite: folks who usually leave Jamaica for a better life abroad send money home to help their families. In my case, Mama was the one sending money, so I had no excuse for not completing my educational program.

From childhood, I recognized my mother's extraordinary nature, and I made a solemn promise to myself: to bring her pride and support her whenever she required it. I resolved to become a nurse, dedicating myself to her care—after all, she was my true champion. I aspired to repay her kindness manifold, to offer her the same selfless devotion she had showered upon me. My opportunity to fulfill this pledge would come.

My Father's brother, Uncle Papa represents
my father Noel Augustus Johnson. They looked alike.

My Mother, Renza (Girly) Bryan.   Lorna, like mother, like daughter.

(L-R) My big brother Warren, Althea, my Grandpa Uriah Bryan,
my younger brother Danny, Aunt Girty and her husband,
Mr. Palmer, and their son Ali and Lorna in front.

Left, is Mama's first son Warren, and his friends.

Mama's fourth child Judith.

Danny, Mama's last son.

(L-R) Danny, Althea, and Lorna.

(L-R) Lorna, Chevron, (Gem's oldest daughter) Althea,
Lor-ren(Gem's youngest).

Mama and all her children
(Lef) Warren, Ionie, Danny,
(Right) Lorna, Judith, and Althea.

Mama's Marriage to Brother Ford.

(L-R) Alice Brown, Lorna, Diane Williams,
Florence Griffith Joyner (Flo-Jo), and husband, Al Joyner.

Lorna, dirt track, Jamaica.   Mt. Sac relays

Lorna singing in the Church Choir 2nd from the right, the front row

Mama on her bicycle.   Horace (Slippy) Mama's nephew.

My mother's sister, Gertrude and Alister Palmer's wedding

Mama and her sister, Mavia Moulton

Mama and Joshua
(Althea's first son) at Salt River.

Lorna and Ionie (Gem).

(L-R) Gem, Althea, and Lorna.　　　Mama, Matt, and Josh,
grandchildren

(L-R Back row) Mama, Loran, Judith
(Front) Althea.

Althea's Wedding
(LR) Chevron, Pete, Gem, Mama, Althea,
Lorna, Lor-ren, Dr. Diop, Paulette, and her son, E.J.

Gem's Wedding (L-R)
Lorna, Pete's Mother, Pete's nephew, Pete, Gem,
Mama Pete's father and, Aunt Vera, my father's sister.

Then Camilla Parker-Bowles, Duchess of Cornwall, Mama, and Lorna
Now, Queen Consort of the United Kingdom.

Then, Prince Charles and Lorna.
Now, Charles III, King of the United Kingdom.

(L-R) Mama, Prime Minister Bruce Golden, Horace Mason, Nephew.

(L-R) Mama, Lorna, and the former Principal of Hayes Primary School.

Lorna and students at Hayes Primary School.

Lorna, receiving an award at USC.
(L-R) Dr. Abdoulaye Diop,
Cynthia Hinds, Hubert Hinds, Lorna, and another awardee at USC.

Mama's 80th Birthday party
(L-R) Ms. Cousins, Lor-ren,
Mama, and Mr. Miller.

Mama's 80th birthday makes the Newspaper.

Mama's grandkids from my brother Warren and Gem.
(L-R)Tamika, Lorna, Gem, and Charmaine.
(Front) Lor-ren in a plaid jacket.

Mama's children and grandchildren.

Mama and her best friend,
Mr. Ormsby.

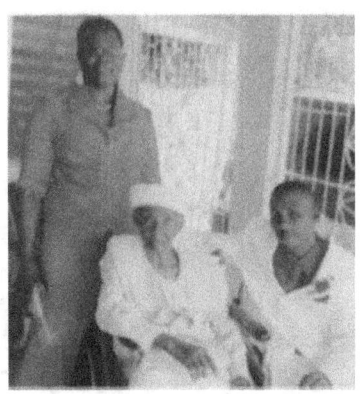

Elaine (Pansy) Beckford,
Mama, and Chiney.

(L-R) Nikiesha, Mr. Miller, and Mama.

Lorna and Mama. Mama and Lorna.

Just Mama.

Chapter Nine

COURAGE TO TRY

"The biggest adventure you can take is to live the life of your dreams."

—*Oprah Winfrey*

A few years after graduating from nursing school, I was recruited to California to work as a registered nurse. I worked full-time and went to school part-time, eliminating the need for student loans and government assistance. I supported myself and worked solely on whatever grants were available to me. I furthered my education and graduated with a B.Sc. from the University of LaVerne in Health Care Management, a Nurse Practitioner certificate, and a Master of Science in Nursing and midwifery with a minor in Finance, from the University of Southern California. I completed my first-year doctoral program at UCLA, still without education debts. Both my older and my youngest sisters did the same thing; they obtained doctoral degrees without student loans. As mom would say, "Working hard never hurts anyone." I was motivated to become the best nurse midwife I could be, and I wanted to make my mother proud.

When I arrived in California as a Registered Nurse recruited from Canada, I had no idea that my life would reach the heights it did. Following in my mother's footsteps, I used my education to help others less fortunate. I saw firsthand the unequal access to healthcare for people of color, and I wanted to work from within to change the system for underserved women, children and people of color.

Armed with my degrees in healthcare management, finance, and nurse midwifery, with the ingenuity and vision of my mom and the support of a great partner, Dr. Abdoulaye Diop, I opened a medical facility in South Central Los Angeles to serve the underserved, underrepresented and marginalized. I chose to work in the inner city because I am my mother's child. Like her, I was eternally grateful for my good fortune, and the sense of purpose she instilled in me paid dividends. I did well enough financially to be able to open additional clinics, which allowed me to serve a wider population. Unexcpected financial gains made it possible for me to venture into real estate including the purchase of my blessed home in Beverly Hills. I would again learn that Mama is always right because that house became my next steppingstone.

I knew as Mama said, without a shadow of a doubt, that a selfless, generous, healthy person goes beyond oneself, and that life is most rewarding when sharing our gifts with others. I have seen how small acts of kindness transformed lives. I have seen how a kind word healed a wounded soul and how financial support turned a would-be delinquent into a hedge fund manager. Giving of spirit is as important as giving of resources but giving of spirit is truly transformative to the receiver and the giver. I don't mean reciprocal altruism. It does not work. Give and expect nothing, at least not from the people you gave to. Blessings, if deserved, may never come from whom you've helped, but it opens your channel for God's grace. Your grace will come from elsewhere, sometimes from the satisfaction of a smile on the face of a life once in distress.

There were times when I climbed the proverbial ladder when I was tired. When I need a safe space and support. Only then did I think to ask who was there for Mama? As a child with a life full of bliss, no one, certainly not me, would think to ask how Mama's life was through her eyes. Who was she on the inside? Before the trials and tribulations, before the betrayal, and before her bravery in surmounting her intrepid spirit? How did she cope with her often interrupted life? I couldn't answer those questions. Regardless, Mama imprinted a legacy worthy of carrying on, and I was glad to have been handed one of those batons.

In 1983, I was at the Sunkist track and field championship meet at the Coliseum Stadium in Los Angeles. A few of my old running buddies were there training for the 1984 Summer Olympics, which were to be held in Los Angeles. As I sat in the stands and watched women run the 100m and 200m, I felt I could do that. I rekindled my love of running and started training with them. Because I'd never had the time to devote to running earlier, my training had been sporadic. I'd run some races in Canada as one of my coaches lived in Vancouver, and I was still a Canadian citizen. There was no question I was a runner, and I was good. I thoroughly enjoyed the power of sports and felt accomplished when I ran.

That chance meet-up in 1983 led me to Jamaica for the 1988, Olympics trials where I qualified as a contender for the track and field Olympic team in Seoul, Korea. I'd run an impressive 11.4 seconds in the 100 meters dash, but the Jamaican women, relentless in their pursuit of excellence, edged me out for first and second spots; however, I did place and qualified for a spot on the team that should have secured me a place for the 4X100 relay team. But because of politics, and my history of running for Canada and not Jamaica, I was denied traveling with the team to Seoul. I would've loved being a part of that history, but alas, as Mama would say, something else was meant for me. Running that summer as teammates with some of the world's best U.S. athletes, Evelyn Ashford, Alice Brown, and Florence Griffin Joyner in the Mount Sac relays was a special moment for me, and a welcome legacy for the Bryan/Johnson family name and Corn Piece.

At the 1988 Olympics trials an incomparable runner clocked in at 10.49 seconds. Indeed, in her one-legged catsuit, the famous Florence Delorez Griffith-Joyner, known as Flo-Jo, and my teammate, left the competition in the dust. I was sitting in the stadium in Kingston, Jamaica, listening to the race on the radio when it was announced she had a non-wind-aided time of 10.49 seconds. Unbelievable. "No way," I said, my hands over my mouth in shock. My 11.4 seconds was in the dust comparatively. Named the fastest woman of all time, Flo-Jo set the world records in the Olympic trials and went on to win gold in Seoul for both the 100 m and 200 m. Her record in the 100 m still stands to this day. I was so proud and happy for her success and the beautiful friend and colleague she was. Sadly, at the age of thirty-eight, the legend died in her sleep during an epileptic episode.

I usually visited Mama several times a year. Now I was home to compete in the Olympic trials as an athlete, and it was nice to go and see her while I was there. One day I turned up wearing a lovely sleeveless summer dress with spaghetti straps. To Mama, I might as well have been naked.

"Where are you going dress like that? Why don't you put clothes on and cover yourself? Why don't you dress properly? I really don't understand how you are on the streets looking like that."

"Like what, Mama? What's wrong with my dress?" Even as an adult, I still had to listen to Mama's complaints about how I chose to dress.

It's Jamaica. It's hot, hot, hot. As Third World sang, it's *96° in the Shade*. It wasn't just me she'd complain about. Whatever city or country we traveled to, seeing people on the streets dressed in skimpy clothing would prompt Mama's comment, "How could people leave their house dressed like that?" Don't bother trying to tell Mama these were modern times. I don't know what she'd have said about First Lady Michelle Obama and her stunning sleeveless outfits!

The importance of being appropriately dressed is not just a Mama thing; it's a cultural thing prevalent throughout Jamaica. While Mama was in the hospital, I wore a sleeveless dress during a visit.

"Good day, Ma'am. How are you doing today? As protocol, we'll have to ask you to please put on a shawl to cover your shoulder before you come into the facility." Even years later that was how I was greeted when I went to visit my mom in the hospital by the staff nurse. The same thing happened at the courthouse. I was told I had to be 'properly clothed' to enter this type of public facility. When in Jamaica I always bring a shawl with me.

As I spent time with Mama over the years, apart from this dress business, I'd come to appreciate how extraordinarily advanced she was for her time and for her community. To this day, I have no idea how she even learned to drive, but if I know anything about Mama that was the least of her challenges. She would find a way to do anything she'd set her mind to.

The significance of my mother's contributions to her community was impressed upon me on one of my trips to Jamaica. A man in a furniture truck stopped me because I was driving Mama's car. When he realized I was not Sister Ford but her daughter, he told me how grateful he was that Mama had taken him under her wing. She had started him in the furniture business and inspired the beginning of his own company. The stories didn't stop there. Whenever I returned home and drove Mama's car in the surrounding areas of our home, I was often stopped. When they realized I was her daughter, they almost always shared stories of how grateful they were for my mom's inspiration and guidance.

In the earlier days of building my business, it was difficult for me to get away so Mama would visit me in California. Knowing how much she loved children, I took her to a Christmas party for the children I served in the inner city of East Los Angeles community. Impressed by my work, she wanted me to come to Jamaica and create a similar program at her church for the children and her seniors. How could I turn her down?

As the head of the Senior Ministry at her church, Mama was proud when I kept my promise. I brought washcloths, toothpaste, soap, and other goodies that she gave away to her church members. I enjoyed doing it, and it made her happy. It was very hard for Mama when the time came for her to turn over her role as leader and caregiver of the church's seniors. Not making a difference in people's lives was difficult.

The church she co-founded acknowledged her contribution with a certificate for the work she'd done over the years and she was so very proud. She kept it at her bedside. Because of Mama's love for the elderly and the young, I hope to one day build a Care Center in her honor. It is so needed.

I've personally watched many elderly people in our community suffer because of limited resources and improper care. I've also watched bright kids end up on the street because they didn't have access to the bare essentials that could make a difference in their lives. My goal was, and is to continue to help the people in the community of Uppa Hill through scholarships and other social programs. My offer to help led me to meet members of the British royalty.

Chapter Ten

LEGACY

"The love of a family is life's greatest blessings."

—*Unknown*

In our family, my mother was the weaver, intricately stitching together love and care to form a mosaic of kinship. With six of us under her wings, she loved us endlessly, yet she still found room in her heart for more, embracing children of other relatives like Chiney as her own. Before him, others found refuge in her nurturing embrace. Our cousin Donovan, Aunty Girty's son was our grandpa's, favorite grandson. Frail and sickly he left a void when he departed this world at the tender age of twelve. Then came Paulette Scarlett, and the irrepressible Slippy, (Horace Mason) my cherished cousin. He was a great mentor to me in my youth and my mom's trusted confidant. So many others found solace in the warmth of Mama's heart, Kirk, Sassy, and others.

When all Mama's children had flown the coup, Chiney was the one who remained at home to oversee much of Mama's care.

As she got older, they grew closer, and he was very protective of her and her husband, and to get to Mama, you had to go through Chiney. His devotion to her proved a blessing and Chiney still lives in our home, picking up where Mama left off, and taking care of my brother Danny.

As with all families, there are tragedies. My mother's relationship with my sister Judith fractured. We believed it happened the day Mama put her on a plane to New York to live with Gem. Angry at not being able to say goodbye to her friends, Judith simply nixed many family members from her embrace over time. To the day Mama died, Judith remained in her heart and she often reminded us to reach out as she was our sister from the same womb.

The men in our family, unfortunately, did not fare well. Many of them died early. My amazing older brother Warren died at the age of thirty-seven from a stroke secondary to hypertension. My father was gone at age forty-two, his first son at thirty-two, and my youngest brother Danny, though still alive, was stricken with mental illness.

In his early 20s, Danny's behavior became erratic and we noticed the first signs of his mental instability. He was later diagnosed with bipolar disorder. Danny was living in Toronto, Canada, with Warren when he got mixed up with a set of bad friends and started doing drugs. We didn't know which came first, the drugs or the disease. It was hard for us to understand why Danny, so outgoing and handsome, was challenged in this way. We always thought his life would be blessed because he was so loving.

Thinking it best to get him out of that environment and to give him a fresh start, I brought Danny to California to live with me. I wanted to help him have a better life and give him the support he needed, medically and otherwise. At first, things were great. Going just swimmingly. Once again, we were just like young siblings–having fun, joking around, and sharing our lives. I love Danny, and I know he loves me. Through a friend, I got him a job at a mechanic shop. He was great at it and loved his work. The guys in the shop liked him too.

Eventually, though, Danny's work began to deteriorate, and he was late or a no-show for work time and time again. He got off his meds and eventually stopped showing up to work at all. Drugs, supplied by someone he'd met at church of all the places were back in the picture. I was never sure what the next phone call would bring and stayed in a state of anxiety.

After a year of living with me, Danny relocated to New York to try once again to rebuild his life with Gem. Married with her husband and two children to consider, no matter how she tried to help him, Danny unwittingly sabotaged all efforts because of his illness. It was hard to be angry with him knowing his illness was a driver, but his relapses were frustrating and infuriating. There were long periods when he didn't come out of his room, suffering from depression and then mania. When manic, he often talked to himself all night long without ever sleeping. There were even times he was physically violent and utterly unaware of what he was doing. This made me question the Bipolar diagnosis. The violence and talking to himself could have been schizophrenia. His unpredictability was both frightening and sad. He'd often be out even in the snow looking for drugs, which was hard for Gem. At some point, it was too much for him to continue living with her. I'm not sure what happened, but Danny ended up again with Warren, who'd moved to Florida.

As long as Danny stayed on his medication, he was fine, but like most people with mental illness will tell you, they'd rather be mad than take zombie-inducing medications. Many turn to street drugs to turn off their perpetually whirling minds, leading to addiction. Short of holding him down and administering the medication ourselves we couldn't do much more for Danny. It broke our hearts as it did, Mama's. We watched and monitored Danny closely, but even that had its limits. Everyone knew to limit the amount of money we gave him, so when he'd ask for a few dollars for cigarettes, we only gave him a few but were never sure if the money was for something else. I hated seeing my brother like this but even medically trained, I could do nothing more.

Danny had gotten to the stage where no one could care for him, so he went back to Jamaica to live with Mama, her husband, and Chiney. Danny and Mama had a very unique relationship, and you could see and feel the love between them. They looked out for each other, and for a while, things went well. Unfortunately, Danny got off his medication again, which proved too much even for Mama to handle. When he flipped out—screaming and arguing the police were called. They took him to the doctor, who gave him a shot to bring him back into balance. They'd have quickly put someone with means like Danny in Bellevue, the mental hospital, but Mama wouldn't have it. She, who had emphasized the importance of family and always being there, once again stepped up.

My mother had a powerful influence on anyone who lived in our house. Her four girls, two of whom have doctorates in education, while the other two are successful businesswomen, are a testament to her love and commitment. The list could go on and on with examples of people who'd made good lives for themselves after learning from my mother's example.

As Mom got older, she accepted life as it came, the wins and challenges—her eldest son's death at thirty-seven years, and now her youngest son challenged by mental illness. She took on Danny's care like a champion, and even as she began experiencing medical problems of her own, she remained concerned about her children's health and well-being. As Mama often explained, *"Whatever happens, there is always something good to be found in it."* Find the good in every situation because God will always protect and care for you. Never fear adversity because it brings with it the seed of an equivalent or greater advantage.

Do the work, rise to the occasion, have faith and courage, and God always brings something good from a challenge. To this day, I'm still grateful for Mama's work ethic and character-building lessons. I'm especially thankful for her lessons on giving because in L.A. I witnessed society's marginalization up close and personal. Everyone can make conscious choices every day, both small and large, to make a difference. It is especially sobering when I know that the world has enough resources to stamp out poverty and enough intellect to tackle the debilitating effects of racism head-on, recognizing it for the selfish act it is.

My birth country, Jamaica, seeded me with confidence and a fighting and giving spirit that helped me to 'become.' To make a difference in another country felt good to me, especially since I'd come to appreciate that we are all connected. My small, beautiful island in the sun was responsible for any success I enjoyed. Having taught me to be keen, innovative, and striving, it trained me to see and take advantage of the opportunities my adopted first-world country afforded. Though my American life has taken me far away from rural Corn Piece to places I never imagined, it was all due to my Jamaica upbringing and Mama's guidance and teachings. In gratitude, I honor George Colman's quote, 'Praise the bridge that carried you over.'

I was eager to share my success with Mama. She'd inspired my life's work to improve the lives of those living in challenged communities. Though my world had crossed over into glitz and glamour, I wanted to introduce Mama to my circle of givers, from colleagues to friends and even to royalty. People all furthering the cause of poverty and equality. I wanted her to see the enormous wings she'd given me and that I had flown and dared to soar.

In 2008, when the opportunity to support a nationwide rollout of computers to schools on the island, I became a benefactor to the project for my Alma Mater, Hayes Primary School in Clarendon. For the kickoff, a big bash was given in Kingston, where several American celebrities such as Cedric the Entertainer, Steve Harvey, and Bill Bellamy rose to the philanthropic challenge and were in attendance. All the school principals receiving computers from around the country traveled to the event. The Honorable Bruce Golding, the prime minister of Jamaica at the time, was in attendance, and I was asked to present the computers to the Principal of my Alma Mater. Always proud that Mama's "giving gene" had rubbed off on me, I had Mama accompany me to the podium to present the award. As she stood regally beside me, beaming with pride, I, too, was never prouder. Mama took it in stride, and it was nice to have a commemorative photograph with the Prime Minister. She cherished that photo, which she hung in her home.

The Royal Family

In 2001, Prince Charles, the Prince of Wales, visited Rose Town, Jamaica at the request of residents. A community, which in the 1950s boasted churches, town halls, libraries, and beautiful homes, it was now considered a no-go zone, an area blighted by years of decay and harrowing violence. The community was despondent. Our beautiful tropical island with its endless sunshine should never see such despair. Four years later, in 2005, Prince Charles Foundation awarded a grant for the redevelopment of Rose Town and I was tapped to be on the Prince's committee. Partnering with local community representatives to rebuild the once-thriving town was right in line with my philanthropic goals. As the project took shape, members of its various committees and I were invited to meet Prince Charles in London for a two-day event at Kensington Palace and Clarence Hall.

A year after we'd been invited to Kensington Palace, which was a few years after the project had begun, the Prince and his wife were scheduled to be on the island to check on the project's progress. I couldn't wait to introduce Mama to Prince Charles and his wife, the Duchess of Cornwall, Camilla, at the kickoff event. I arranged for a driver to take Mama and me on the three-hour excursion to the Rose Hall Great House in Montego Bay, where the event was being held.

I was surprised that Rose Hall was the event's venue, as the Half-Moon property just down the road in MoBay, with its stunning coasts, was a favorite of the Royals when on the island. This was where I had imagined the Royals would be staying rather than at the Great House, which, though beautifully refurbished, had a harrowing history. Rose Hall was once a slave plantation and the place where its owner Annie

Palmer allegedly killed all three of her husbands. The folktale, *The White Witch of Rose Hall* was one every child knew. There was even a ditty, "The Ballad of Annie Palmer," recorded by Johnny Cash, who owned the property next door. And legend has it she still haunts the property.

Mama and The Duchess stuck up a conversation. They both loved hats, and for my mom, the more colorful, the better. Always perfectly dressed, this day was no different. The Duchess commented on Mama's vibrant accessories and sense of style, which under most circumstances would have made my mother proud. But that day, Mama was different. Mama was shy when the Duchess complimented her on her fashion. And when Prince Charles tried to make conversation, she seemed reticent and a little disengaged. I just couldn't get her to connect, though both Prince Charles and his wife loved her. Mama reciprocated their feelings only with her beautiful, shy, far-away smile.

Watching the women together, it suddenly struck me that Mama, most likely, had gotten her love of hats from the Brits of her day! When she was born in 1931, Jamaica mimicked British styles, traditions, and values. These hand-me-down protocols shaped Jamaica's perspectives and habits, some remaining to this day. I mean, who wears a felt beret as part of a school uniform in 90-plus-degree heat? Most Jamaican schools did until the mid-70s!

Watching them, I flashed back to earlier times. Mama had always reminded me of a Queen, especially seeing her alight from her car, strut down the street, hips swinging gracefully, handbag hanging over her wrist and a hat perched on her head or a scarf tied under her chin, much like Queen Elizabeth does when riding at Balmoral.

Even many years after they met, when I got Christmas greetings from the Royals, they always asked about my Mama. But this humble woman, my Jamaican Queen, the reason I became the woman I am; my champion, with her ever-so-sweet smile, and gentle eyes that shined bright and tender, who had blessed others was slipping away.

It was at the event at Rose Hall that I first noticed the change. Distracted by the excitement, I was remiss in addressing it, and eager to move on to the other events with the Royals, I let it slide. But after meeting Prince Charles and The Duchess, my mother didn't want to stay and socialize. She insisted on going home, repeating over and over that she needed to check in on Brother Miller, her third husband. My stepfather, Brother Ford, had long passed. Since there were helpers at home and Brother Miller was not an invalid but was in fact quite a sturdy man, I couldn't fathom why Mama was so insistent. She was relentless, adamant that she she needed to go home to make sure he had enough to eat, and her doggedness annoyed me quite a bit.

Thinking back, I guess I should've understood her protectiveness. Ten years after her blissful wedding, and about a year after I left Jamaica for Canada, Brother Ford died suddenly from a diabetic coma. He'd always been strict with his diet and made sure he was in tip-top shape. We'd never seen him sick and so never imagined he would die so early. The irony was the doctor later said that if he'd eaten a piece of candy, it could have saved his life. Once again, Mama had been alone, now with six children, the youngest only six years old.

She was fiercely protective of Brother Miller and could never live with the thought of losing a third husband. Perhaps worry had led to an anxiety attack. Or it could have been the eerie location of the event. In those days no one died of natural causes. Death was always for some nefarious reason. And some of the mean folks in the village had accused her of causing her husband's death. Still, her behavior, even considering the legend of Rose Hall, struck me as very strange.

My mother loved her car and it wasn't unusual that she was uncomfortable with someone else driving it, but that night she seemed downright paranoid. She was focused on the driver who'd dropped us off, believing he was taking her car for a joy ride. I'd let it go, but her unyielding demands forced me to cut the evening short to get her home. I simply had to get her out of there, if for no other reason than to get a break from her incessant nervousness. I'd planned such a great night for us, and was so disappointed.

I should've known something was seriously wrong. There had been signs even earlier that I'd also missed or didn't want to see. Some were small things, insignificant, while others were glaring. I'd left Jamaica as a teenager, and although my visits home were frequent, without the benefit of continually observing the changes in her habits, movements, attitudes, and daily activities, until that day, I attributed them to her getting older.

Chapter Eleven

WANDERING

"I know God will not give me anything I can't handle.
I just wish He didn't trust me so much."

—*Mother Teresa of Calcutta*

Mama had worked her entire life. We were always afraid of what would happen once she stopped. She still seemed to enjoy her daily routine and craved activities to occupy her perpetually working mind. She'd lived a full life up until then and always loved to travel. Gradually, though, Mama found more and more excuses why she couldn't leave her home to visit her children in the U.S. Mama's farm raised chickens for the chicken processing plant, Jamaica Broiler. It took about six to eight weeks for the chickens to mature, and then they would be collected by the plant trucks, and she'd ready things for the next batch of chickens to arrive. Usually, Mama would travel to see her children or go on various outings with the church in-between deliveries, but no longer.

I'd always loved it when Mama came to California, and I know Gem loved it when she came to New York. However, Mama began insisting she couldn't visit anymore because she had the chickens and was waiting for a new delivery, which was eight or more weeks away! In hindsight, it was another indication that the disease had taken hold much earlier than we'd thought.

Just before the new millennium in 2000, Mama got caught up in the frenzy, along with everyone else that the world would end, something we couldn't imagine our independent thinker of a mother would ever do. It was around this same time that she did something else completely out of character.

Years earlier, she'd given me a piece of land. Gem and I talked about our desire to build a house on it someday. I'd long been sending money to Mama to set aside for a house-building fund. During our many conversations, Gem and I mentioned that the three of us would design and build the house together when the time came. Only we hadn't finalized anything with Mama.

About three or four months after our last conversation about it, Mama called to tell us she'd taken the money from the bank account and built a house! We couldn't believe it. How does one build a house in four months? Not only that, I was also with her only a few months earlier and she never discussed it, so how could this be? Gem and I were furious. You don't build a quality home in that short timeframe in Jamaica or anywhere else in the world, for that matter. This was not our typical Mama—hear something, do something. No. Something was off. First, the money was not hers to spend. It was my money, and the land, I thought we'd agreed, she'd given it to me. Mama under normal circumstances would never have done that without consulting me. But to our surprise, Mama had done just that without any of us knowing.

Even people in the community said they'd never seen a house built so fast. What we found out the next time we visited was just how right we were: it was not a quality home. It had incorporated some of our ideas but was not well built. And there was nothing we could do to fix it. I always knew my mom to be strong-willed, but this was out of character, even for her. Eventually, we rented out the house.

On reflection, I suspect Mama already knew something was wrong. Eventually, she admitted to losing her capacity and often said, "I'm losing my memory, and I want you guys to come and take care of me because I can't do many things anymore. You need to come and take over." In her less rational mind, she'd thought if she built the house, her children would come home.

Even as a medical professional, I wasn't trained in, nor had prior experience with Alzheimer's to identify that she'd already transitioned into early dementia. If my assumptions were correct, Mama was in her late sixties when it started. Albeit at a turtle's pace, everything began to change.

On September 16, 2004, Hurricane Ivan decimated parts of the Caribbean and the USA. When it hit Jamaica, it demolished Mama's chicken farm. We'd already wanted her to stop working so hard when she turned seventy, so now at seventy-three, we thought this catastrophe would finally make her retire. Although the hurricane destroyed the farm and vagabonds stole much of her equipment, it was not enough to stop Mama from working. We suggested that she consider immigrating to be near us. No such luck. Mama dug in her heels and swore she wouldn't leave no matter how we insisted.

Returning to California, after a visit I began to keep in touch more regularly. To my mind, and from my memories of talking to her in person and over the phone, Mama was her, normal self most of the time. She heard what she wanted to hear and blocked out things she didn't want to address, which was nothing new. She was still running her chicken farm and serving as a senior citizen group leader at her church. Then a new crisis took the spotlight off her.

In 2006 my sister Gem was diagnosed with colon cancer. This was another blow for Mama, who'd already experienced enormous losses during her life. It was then that I learned my mother had lost a child—Warren's twin brother. When she'd first married Papa and got pregnant, she was expecting twins. Unfortunately, the nurse who cared for her during the pregnancy was not around at the time of delivery, and the substitute nurse, who'd come to oversee the delivery, was not informed that Mama was carrying twins. So, when Warren arrived, she cut the umbilical cord and delivered the placenta, thinking it was all over, but shortly, they realized there was another baby who it turned out was stillborn or had died shortly after his eventual birth.

I can only imagine how strong Mama had to have been to take care of her new husband, and her new baby, build businesses, grieve, and manage the regret and anguish of losing a baby when it could have been prevented. I wondered if she felt any responsibility for not informing the nurse that she was carrying twins, but she was only nineteen years old.

I also remember the day one of Mama's church sisters, Miss Daphne, was having a baby. It appeared to be a difficult birth and someone had called on my mother for help. Immediately, Mama jumped in her car, hurried to the woman's side, and took her to the hospital. Several hours later, when she returned,

I heard three sounds, similar to those I remembered hearing when my father died. Something had gone wrong and Miss Daphne died in the hospital after delivering twins. Both babies had survived. I'm sure it brought back lots of painful memories.

Mama drove the coffin in the back of her car from the funeral to the gravesite while we walked behind. Our Sunday school class choir sang:

> "...*around the throne of God in heaven*
> *thousands of children stand.*
> *Children whose sins are all forgiven*
> *a holy happy band...*
> *singing glory, glory, glory....*"

Mama encouraged the father to seek comfort in a closer relationship with God. He soon started to come to church with us, and later, he and the twins were baptized with her encouragement. Mama was the godmother to the children and even helped to raise them. I believe she didn't have time to be close to too many people because she was busy helping dozens in her community. She'd lost a mother, a son, a stillborn baby, two husbands, and her favorite sister Aunt Girty, and now she was about to lose her eldest daughter.

When my Aunt Mavis told me the story, I asked how my mother handled all of it. Her reply was, "Oh, your mother was a trooper. She is a strong woman."

Unbeknownst to me, my Aunt Mavis was dying at the time from breast cancer, having refused to have an operation. This still brings tears to my eyes because I can identify with my mother and Aunt Mavis. Even a strong woman needs support and someone to confide in. I find enormous similarities between myself and Mama because many people think I'm so strong and don't need support. However, I'm human and like all of us, I need a shoulder to cry on sometimes especially when tough times inevitably arrive. I empathize with how hard things must have been for Mama and how she had to overcome so many obstacles to keep herself going. Where did my mom go for refuge? To whom did she talk? Who did she confide in? Who held her space like she held ours?

Aunt Mavis said Mama's best friend in all the world was her sister, my Aunt Girty. Unfortunately, Aunt Girty had died in 1995 at age fifty-nine. With her best friend and baby sister gone, who was there for her now?

I became a little more involved in Mama's affairs when she agreed to share records and accounts for some of her businesses. Naturally, I got only what she felt I needed. While spending time together, I could now see firsthand all the changes happening to my mother. Once she hid her keys and couldn't remember where they were. She hid her money and her purse and began locking everything up. She was becoming very aggressive, calling people names, including her husband and me. She would accuse people of stealing. Not even I escaped her paranoia. I began to appreciate what was happening, but I couldn't help but feel hurt. There was no reason to hide anything from me or be afraid. I would never do anything to affect my mother negatively. Mama was handling all my finances and business affairs in Jamaica and so since she handled quite a bit of my finances, it was illogical for her to not trust me. Her husband, who was always looking out for her, was now, too, seen as someone stealing from her. How could Mama say something like that about the man who'd looked out for her for over thirty years and, who had done everything for her? "Mama, where are you going?" I would wonder. It was all becoming clearer…Mama was ill.

Mama, who'd never trusted anyone with her business, finally confided to my sister, Gem, and me, that she was no longer capable anymore and wanted to show us everything she had. She constantly tried to bribe us to come back home to live with her, even promising us bigger portions of her estate. It became clear to us why in her mind she had justified building the house! After going through my mom's finances, my sister and I chuckled. Her businesses, fantastic by Jamaican standards and cost of living, could not compare to how well we were all doing in our businesses in the U.S.

I didn't know precisely what was occurring in Mama's brain, but experiencing the changes was hard for me. I surmised that Mama had been living with some form of Alzheimer's for several years but was now in rapid decline. As she moved swiftly toward the terminal stages five and six the signs became more pronounced as she increasingly lost her ability to perform basic daily tasks. All the changes I'd noticed in the previous years, I'd simply chalked up to her becoming a more hard-headed, stubborn woman in her old age. Now she was immovable and stubborn as an ox. There was no way to convince her to leave Jamaica and return to the U.S. with me.

In Jamaica, Mama was large and in charge. She was the boss, the big lady; everyone came to her for help—a big fish in a small pond. In the U.S., she was like a baby and didn't know what to do. And what of her husband, she'd inquire. On several occasions, even before her illness, we'd tried to convince Mama to relocate with us to the States. Gem had even applied for her green card in the early 90s, which was granted but allowed to lapse. Mama was a woman of the Jamaican soil, a true *yardie*, as we would say, and that's where she would remain. But now that things were changing, and there was no denying that Mama's once brilliant, sharp, colorful mind was little by little dying, what would we do?

Mama oscillated between lucidity and loss. On one of the days when Mama was *corpus mentis,* she faced yet another loss. I knew many people in our community loved Mama; however, I don't remember her having a close friend. In talking to Aunt Mavis, her only living sister, I learned that after Aunt Girty died Mama confided in the church's pastors, ministers, and other high-ranking officials including Mrs. Stewart a Justice of the Peace (JP) and Principal of Vere Technical High School my Alma mater. At least she had spiritual comfort. The prospect of losing Gem was not something I believe Mama could face. Gem had always been her favorite—the one she'd charged with being her eyes and ears, who made sure we were taken care of in our respective foreign lands. So, it was to Gem to whom Mama wanted to entrust her business.

After her first bout with cancer, Gem, unable to take on the responsibility encouraged Mama to name me her executor. Mama resisted, which led me to believe she didn't fully understand the gravity of Gem's illness. In denial or in and out of dementia, Gem and I finally had to sit with Mama to convince her that because of my business experience and being her daughter, rather than strangers, I was the best to manage her affairs. After many conversations, we were able to convince her that Cousin Slippy, (Horace)her trusted nephew, would help me to manage her affairs and she agreed.

In 2006, during my sister's first battle with cancer, nothing could've pulled me away from her side. With no regrets, I chose to leave my love partner, Dr. Abdoulaye Diop in California to move to New York to be with her. When her colon cancer returned in 2010, I knew I had to be with her again. This time the cancer had spread, and the prognosis was poor. There was nothing that could keep me away.

Gem's final wish was to see Mama one last time. With Mama in Jamaica and her in New York and Mama's insistence she didn't want to see her in the hospital, I had a battle on my hands. Gem demanded that even if I had to go to Jamaica, I needed to bring Mama to her. She must see her before she passed.

"There is nothing I can do for her. I don't want to go. There is nothing I can do, and I'm not leaving my husband." Mama kept saying, over and over. Had I looked beyond the surface words, I would've recognized her fear of losing her daughter. Maybe this was one loss too many, and Mama couldn't find the strength to face the inevitable. Her stubbornness, which had trickled down to me, made me more determined to get her to the U.S. to see Gem. This was certainly not the Mama I or any of us knew.

I agreed with my Aunt that my mother was a trooper, and I believe she was in a good place even with Alzheimer's and dementia. I'd sometimes wonder, though, if loss had finally caught up with her. Was this Alzheimer's a way to finally tamp down all the pain she'd endured silently? Was this her time not to be responsible for the entire world anymore and just find peace in her absence of mind? One of the spiritual leaders trying to comfort me when I was distraught explained that the soul never dies, and because Mama was such a strong soul, she would never settle for less no matter what life.

I finally decided to fly to Jamaica. When I got there, Mama's passport was nowhere to be found, and she was still refusing to come with me. She seemed overly concerned about her husband, so I worked with Brother Miller to make sure he told her it was okay to go and see her child. Mama kept saying she couldn't come to see Gem, and though in part I blamed Mama's illness, honestly, I was furious and galled she'd utter such words. I was especially upset one day while talking to Gem on the phone. In the background, Mama could be heard saying she couldn't come to New York. I felt for my sister and was ashamed and heartbroken. I didn't know how to react. No matter how aware of Mama's illness, I found it hard to appreciate that anything would keep her from her dying child. I had to catch myself when the recurring blame game started playing in my head, wondering if she was being a mean old lady. I even questioned if she was doing this to get back at us for not coming home to live with her. Was this payback? I knew it wasn't, but I just couldn't fathom this disease that was robbing her of her humanity.

At the time, I thought Mama might have thrown her passport away as she hadn't planned on traveling anymore. This meant I had to get a new passport and only had a few days to do so. In the past, if one lost a passport, replacing it was simple—fill out a few forms. Since all the necessary information was already in the system, one would get a quick replacement. No more. Now the process required a birth certificate, which my mom had lost eons before, and it was going to be an involved, arduous, and time-consuming process. Time was running out for Gem, and my sister kept calling, asking what was taking so long to get back with Mama to the hospital. Even while Gem was dying, she still ran the ship and gave orders.

Though crestfallen, my sister, beautiful and wise to the very end, was more aware and compassionate than I. She was able to look beyond Mama's words to her fear. "Don't get so upset, Lorna. Mama's not in her right mind. Keep trying. She'll come. Please find a way to bring her to my bedside. I *need* to see her one last time."

Gem was so understanding. And as always, she was right. In reality, my Mama, too, was very sick. Because I was so close to Gem, it was painful for me. We all knew Gem was special to Mama. She would be with me most of the time when I'd go to Jamaica. If she weren't, the first thing out of Mama's mouth would be, "Where is Gem?" I'd often tease Mama that she loved Gem more than she loved me, and she would just brush me away. "Aren't you happy to see me, at least?" She would just laugh. I should've understood it would have been as hard a time for Mama as it was for me.

I was scared my sister would die before I made it back to see her and felt caught between a rock and a hard place. The doctor had told me we might only have days before we lost Gem. When I spoke to her, she wanted me to come back right away, so I left my Mama in Jamaica and asked Cousin Slippy, who was like a big brother, to take over from me with the passport and plan to travel with Mama.

Miraculously we were able to make this happen. Now we had to get a replacement visa. Luckily, I had a relationship with the U.S. Administration. I made a phone call to the White House for help and within twenty-four hours, I was able to get Mama a visa. I flew back and was vigilantly by my sister's bedside, praying for a miracle. Mama and Horace arrived shortly after I'd returned. It was all coming full circle because it was Mama's teachings which lead to my relationship with the White House in the first place.

I had long since expanded a successful business and chain of medical clinics serving South Central Los Angeles and became a real estate investor, which allowed me to pay it forward. In keeping with my mother's teaching, "to whom much is given, much is required," I was ready to give back, and so started a foundation dedicated to helping women and children globally, particularly youth ages six through twenty-two. Bringing together my talents for business, sports, health, and education, I hoped to support and help fulfill dreams often shattered in underserved communities.

I regularly held fundraisers for various charities with influencers and change agents at my home in Beverly Hills. At one such event, attended by government officials and a number of democratic fundraisers I was asked and agreed to do a fundraiser for a young presidential hopeful named Senator Barack Obama. Though I'd never leaned on my people or asked for anything in return, I decided to involve all my friends and they were only too happy to support in raising funds for his candidacy. To be honest, at that time, I had no real idea how the fundraising world worked at that level. Pioneering community-builder and consultant Lena Kennedy allowed me to shadow her, and I started working with her to learn the ropes. With headliner then-President of the L.A. City Council Eric Garcetti's support we hosted a wonderful event for our nation's first Black President.

During his first term in office, I learned a lot about the process. I'd become a big-time supporter on the L.A. fundraising scene and began doing more and more events at my home.

Fast forward to 2012 and Obama's bid for a second term: I am now a veteran. I receive a call from Michael Gilmore, the local finance person on the Obama team asking if I'd consider hosting another event for the president, which I was more than happy to do. Michael was very kind, and we'd hit it off at once. The event was outstanding and we'd raised a significant amount of money. There was never a prouder moment in my life than when Barack Obama became the 44th President of the United States of America, and that he would have the chance to serve four more years. Whatever small part I could have played, I had been ready.

I was invited to serve as a member of the Health Committee and National Finance Committee for the Obama campaign. I was later appointed to the President's Advisory Committee on the Arts at The John F. Kennedy Center for the Performing Arts where another most rewarding moment blessed my life. I was able to influence the long-overdue nomination of Ms. Cicely Tyson, an icon and someone I'd come to hold dear, for the Kennedy Center Honors. One day I received a call from Ms. Tyson's assistant who put Ms. Tyson on the line. "You are an angel," said elated. "They have been trying for over twenty years to have me receive this award and you made it happen." I was speechless. I'd worked hard to make it happen and was honored and humbled she'd taken the time to acknowledge it.

Philanthropy and community involvement had led me to this place. Joining forces and collaborating with like-minded people is a fast track to change and growth. The friendships and connections I made throughout the years with the Obama administration proved invaluable in helping my mother and sister. I will forever be grateful to my wonderful friends at the

White House, including Ambassador Ron Kirk, and Julianna Smoot, who were responsible for getting my mother to the United States before my sister passed.

When Mama saw Gem in her hospital bed, she wasn't positive it was her eldest daughter. Her "Gem," (it was she who had given her this nickname) was frail and cachectic, wasting away. Cancer had taken away much of her physical abilities, and death was written all over her. Mom walked over to Gem's bedside, took her hand, and in her typical fashion, began to pray. It was a prayer that could bring anyone to tears. It was like she was her usual self again, alert, clear, and mindful of what was happening around her, if only for a moment. When she was done, she anointed my sister, her daughter, with oil and said, "You are in God's hands in Jesus' name, amen." She then walked away and said, "It is time for me to go now. There is nothing else I can do. I'm leaving now."

And just like that, she was ready to go back to Jamaica. The veil had fallen again as though she wanted to shut out reality. I couldn't understand it. She'd seemed so lucid and loving one moment then suddenly she was simply leaving her dying child behind. I know that was not my mother. The Mama I know would never have uttered such words. She would have stayed and prayed with her daughter until the very end.

While Mama was still in the U.S., I wanted my younger sister Judith to see Gem before she died and reconcile. Perhaps a continuation of her displeasure with our mom, the feud between Gem and Judith had spilled over to almost everyone in our immediate family. She and Mama been estranged for over ten years and it was a source of great pain for Mama. I wanted them all to reconcile, to have no regrets.

Judith was afraid to make the first move, but finally agreed to come. Family had to come first, no matter what. Gem was pleased to see her and I left them to share a private moment. It seems they were able to resolve some of the hurt and pain between them, and when Judith returned, she said nice things about their visit. After ten years away, my sister was back in the picture. It was a bittersweet reunion. It took Gem's death to make it happen.

Phone Call From President Obama

One day while I was in the hospital, I received a call from my friend Michael Gilmore, now Obama's deputy finance director, telling me to stand by for a call from the President. Thinking it was our usual monthly conference call, I was overwhelmed, when Michael told me that the President had heard about Gem and wanted to call personally. I fought back tears. This was a personal call from the President of the United States, Barack Obama, this giant of a man who genuinely loves people, with condolences for our family. When he got on the phone, the President told me he was aware of my sister's situation and that he and Michelle were so very sorry. He wanted me to know that I shouldn't hesitate to ask if there was anything they could do. He then spoke to my sister. She was so far gone, but I knew from her expression how pleased she was because she adored him and was so proud of his presidency. I was touched and humbled.

The beautiful thing was that Mama was present when the call came. Unfortunately, it was one of the days when the veil was drawn. Yet, this moment was hers too. That her dying daughter was speaking to the leader of the free world meant nothing to her, yet it was all because of her.

Gem passed away a few days later. I thank God Cousin Slippy was able to help get Mama to the U.S. in time. And, I'm glad we were able to keep her here until my sister's homegoing. As family members arrived for the service, Mama clearly recognized them, happy to lay eyes on relatives she hadn't seen in a long time. It was great to see her animated again, even on such an unhappy occasion.

Chapter Twelve

CIRCLE OF LIFE

*"Being deeply loved by someone gives you strength
while loving someone deeply gives you courage."*

—*Lao Tzu*

Sadly, Mama declined rapidly once my sister passed. I think that somewhere inside of her, she knew all was not well with her children. After the funeral, Mama went back to Jamaica with my cousins. Soon thereafter, I flew back to see her to make sure everything at home was in good order as the entire family responsibility was now left to me. On my arrival, I noticed Mama had gathered several of Gem's photos and lined them up on her dresser. It broke my heart because I felt, that despite Alzheimer's, without a doubt, she'd realized that my sister, her eldest daughter, was gone.

It was clear she was in and out of lucidity, and there were times she didn't even recognize Gem in the pictures. I think she recognized me as a person in her life, but not necessarily as her daughter. She would look at me, smile, and keep on moving.

When I walked into the room, there was almost no spark of connection in her eyes. Often in and out of *corpus mentis*, there were times when she didn't even recognize her husband.

With Gem gone, I had to deal with the changes occurring with Mama alone. Simultaneously dealing with the loss of my sister and now possibly the loss of Mama whose mental status was precipitously declining right before my eyes, I went into a funk. I'd lost my sister, my sidekick, the family's matriarch-in-waiting, and someone I'd entirely depended on. We were the dream team. In the months following Gem's death, I swung between a range of emotions. I felt utterly alone and confused, simply floating through life as best I could.

Still in disbelief that I'd lost my sister, and not knowing what else to do, I consciously made Mama my priority. I became her go-to person with little or no help.

Mama went back to her antics. She remained active as best she could and was still driving! But as time wore on, she started to drive so slowly that she blocked traffic. Granted, older drivers generally tend to drive slowly. What she called "cautious," however, amounted to hair-pulling danger for herself, other drivers, and me. Mama could no longer manage even basic driving tasks like remaining on the correct side of the road. When I suggested she stop driving, she quipped, "You think I don't know how to drive? I've been driving since *me eye de a mi knee, and I never had an accident that was my fault.* So, I know what I'm doing. Just leave me alone. Everybody in the community knows me. The police know me, and nobody will bother me. They are going to take care of me. They know who I am. I'm big around here, you know—I'm very big around here and everybody know who I am, so I'll be just fine." We could not get Mama to budge no matter how hard we tried.

Against our wishes, Mama drove until January 2011, few months shy of her eightieth birthday. She was not pleased when we finally took her driver's license away. Her car, which had graduated over the years and was now a red Mitsubishi Pajero SUV, was her means of staying connected to the community. She'd long had a telephone, but rather than call someone, Mama would jump into the car to do whatever she needed. As someone who would never retire, how would she get around? What would she do with all of her energy? What would she do without being of daily service to her community? I, too, couldn't imagine the day she would have to stop her life's work and service to her community. So much so, that we thought it would never come.

But in January of 2011, Mama's insurance finally expired and cousin Horace now Mama's insurance broker and a big deal himself, well respected in the community, adamantly refused to renew her license. "No way. No way whatsoever," he said. He wouldn't even consider renewing her insurance with a specialty clause limiting her driving to the district. Mama was livid, but Horace was steadfast. He wanted to protect my Mama and his aunt, as well as the other people on the road. Though not what she wanted to hear, Horace was a no-nonsense kind of fellow (a family trait), and he put his foot down. Mama had no other choice.

With marching orders to get a driver, Mama was, as usual, defiant and drove another three months with no insurance or license! It wasn't until we told her she would go to jail that she started using a driver. Since she still didn't use the telephone to communicate, the transition was difficult. It was almost like we were forcing her to retire. We were also concerned that she might deteriorate further without the ability to come and go. Our concern came to fruition.

By this time, Mama had become a shell of herself with little or no connection to me. She was nearing the terminal stages of Alzheimer's, and we didn't know how much longer she would be with us. We would undoubtedly lose her soon. Worse, it felt like part of her had already gone. A thought consoled me during this difficult time. My spiritual belief is in universal connection. I believe we are all spiritual being; souls living in physical bodies, having a human experience. We are a perfect example of infinite power, evenly distributed in us all with massive energy in sync with the vibrational speed of the Spirit flowing through us. The body is the manifestation of physical movement. As we alter the vibration of our body, everything changes. We are all tri-human beings manifested in Spirit, intellect, and the physical: a perpetual transmutation of energy. I took comfort in my belief that the Spirit is omnipresent. So, Mama will live on because her soul will never die.

I visited more often. It was difficult to reason with Mama now and even harder not to feel hurt when she didn't realize I was her daughter. At times, I was numb, more concerned about providing the care Mama deserved. While a big responsibility, I didn't see it as a burden or liability but rather as an asset of great value. I'm a nurse. I was blessed to have been able to care for my big brother when he had a stroke and died a year later at the age of thirty-seven. I was blessed to have been able to care for my sister until she died at fifty-seven. I feel proud to have been able to take care of my mother until her death at eighty-two years old. It was not easy, but it was my obligation to a woman who deserved the best exit possible and I did what had to be done with gratitude that I was capable.

I came to believe caregivers experienced bigger challenges than the person with dementia. They are constantly searching for signs that the afflicted are still with us. My mother appeared completely detached from life. No longer did she have to listen to the few naysayers spouting that she was the cause of her two husbands' deaths. Her declaration that she would not bury another husband was part of her fear of coming to America. She no longer had to listen to the people who believed payback was certain as the consequences of a life lived.

In my life, my mom had been my North Star on a dark night. She had been dependable as the moon, fiery and sometimes as scorching as the midday sun, while other times as calming as the still water. She deserved all of my effort and care.

My mother's complete detachment from life may have been a gift. Her life had been marred by too many tragedies. Not having to recall them must have been a relief. In a way, I was glad she was unable to remember. As she said, every adversity brings the seed of an equivalent advantage.

Chapter Thirteen

THE FINAL ACT

*"Whoever is careless with the truth in small matters
cannot be trusted with important matters."*

—*Albert Einstein*

It was hard to believe that my mother, larger than life, would ever get old. But here she was nearing eight score and ten! I wanted to do something special to pay homage to her and for the extraordinary life she'd afforded me. To be honest, I think the celebration was more for me and to share with the community that I missed. I wanted to celebrate her that day, and I wanted them to celebrate her as well because my mother had done so much for her children, her church, and her community. Now that she could no longer give as much of her time, people truly began to realize her enormous contribution to their lives and the change in the neighborhood was undeniably noticed.

There was a school close to our home on government land that bordered our front yard. My mother always cleared the area so the kids would have a place to play. After she got ill and couldn't do it anymore, it fell into neglect and turned into a bushy knoll. As her children, people expected us to continue the tradition of upholding the community, but we could do very little as we didn't live there.

I'm not sure how much Mama understood about my wanting to celebrate her eightieth birthday, but I knew I had to do something big. My mom had always loved African music because of its drums and its rhythmic cadence, which reminded her of her church's African influence. I had taken her to one of my favorite hotels in Jamaica the year before to attend a show. She seemed to thoroughly enjoy one particular African band, and although she didn't approve of dancing (unless it was in church) I was shocked when she encouraged me to get on stage to dance with the performers. As she put it, "Go up there and show them what you can do." She, of course, was referring to the Pukkumania dances I'd learned as a child. As a kid she'd loved to watch me dance. Even if she thought some of the moves were silly, it made her laugh. I was less shocked when I recalled that people with Alzheimer's regress to earlier long-term memory, as short-term memory slips away.

When it was time to plan Mama's birthday party, I hired that same band to play. The event took place at the community center playground where we played sports as kids. My brother Warren was a great soccer player, we used to call him Pele. I did track races there as a child: jump racing in crocus bags, fifty-yard races, and the like. It brought back lots of positive childhood memories.

And so, on Mama's 80th birthday, dressed to the nines in one of her favorite colors, we threw a lavish party worthy of the life she'd lived. With food provided for the whole neighborhood, and a giant cake (not your ordinary everyday sheet cake but a 'table' cake about three feet by four feet in size), we celebrated in grand style. It felt wonderful to share her special day with the people she cared for and looked after, and Mama seemed happy.

As the music played, she sat next to her husband, shaking her head to the music. My niece, Lor-ren, and I couldn't resist pulling her up from her chair to dance, which I think she enjoyed, though she tried to resist. At one point she actually got up and danced with the band. I was thrilled and grinning from ear to ear. Somewhere in there was my mother, my champion. She had loosened up and changed her ways as she grew older, maybe because of Alzheimer's. I was the one given an incredible gift: I got to watch Mama smile, dance, and enjoy the celebration of her life. No one deserved it more. My mother's life at that moment gave me pause. It made me look at my own life.

Being there with her gave me a different perspective. I paused, and yes, I looked over my life's accomplishments. We work, we live feverishly, and it all seems like one task or goal after another. We seldom stop and appreciate all we've accomplished—not from a personal, boastful place, but from one of value. It's so much easier to focus on our missteps and failings than our successes. Did we make a difference in our connected world? Were there footprints or a blueprint of our legacy that are immortal for the generations to come? We are here for a reason and taking time to understand whether or not that reason has been fulfilled is living on purpose.

I was always uncomfortable when people carried on about the things I'd done. I think I was always chasing my mother: her love (a word she almost never said), her approval. Her love was in the doing, even when it felt rock hard. It wasn't until

I began traveling the world that I found clarity in my life. I saw the impact of my efforts when I worked on the re-election campaign for President Obama; I saw the impact in other places from the inner city of East Los Angeles to Jamaica to Africa. I learned not to minimize my contributions, to accept that my life added value to others and that that life was no small feat. To provide as much value as I did to a cause I believed in (Obama, giving to kids in my backyard and Africa) felt like something big. And it was. Looking back, it was a big...deal, as Joe Biden would say, and I acknowledged it. What a fantastic feeling, it was not just about making Mama proud—it was also about becoming more comfortable in my space and acknowledging my successes and blessings. After this realization, while spending time with Mama, I began to feel more comfortable with the praise. This was yet another opportunity to continue to grow and learn from my mother.

Through Mama, I learned it was not about me but service to others and impacting lives. She knew who she was and never allowed anyone to define her. She had a powerful mind, and she taught me that we are all born with this fire inside of us if only we dare to find it. Many of us are scared the fire will decimate us, so we don't try.

As a young girl of fifteen, I'd gone out into the world to find my way. I'd thought I needed to find my fire, but the funny thing is I had already found it the day the Angel walked into our house and left us a new baby. I'd become a nurse-midwife, a businesswoman, an entrepreneur, and a philanthropist. I, like Mama, saw a need and tried to rise to the challenge of fulfilling it. I give Mama a lot of credit for her influence on my life. She did what she wanted to do, and so did I. Being with Mama, I was learning to understand myself and my challenges in life. I leaned into her wisdom.

Mama used her mind and her creativity to achieve all she had. If a woman from her time and circumstances, faced with her struggles and losses could make it on her own, then the sky is *not* the limit for the rest of us. It's merely a single spot along our journey to being the best version of ourselves and finding the purpose God intended for us. I believe that.

Chapter Fourteen

ASCENSION

"Aging is a staircase—the upward ascension of the human spirit, bringing us into wisdom, wholeness, and authenticity. As you may know, the entire world operates on a universal law: entropy, the second law of thermodynamics. Entropy means that everything in the world, everything, is in a state of decline and decay, the arch. There's only one exception to this universal law, and that is the human spirit, which can continue to evolve upwards."

—*Jane Fonda*

A year later, Mama faced her ultimate challenge when a stroke left her immobilized. It tested my faith to its limits. When the doctor delivered the prognosis that she might never walk again, I found myself grappling with doubt. How could Mama, the embodiment of resilience, be confined to immobility? Raised in the unwavering belief that God's presence was ever at hand, I sought solace in my faith, clinging to the hope of a miraculous recovery.

I couldn't bear the thought of losing her, not so fast and especially in such a debilitating manner. Despite the veil, which shielded her from some of the emotional anguish, witnessing her physical suffering was agonizing. She deserved a serene departure from this world. While I knew her spirit would endure, forever intertwined with mine, I had to confront the harsh reality that her physical presence was waning.

Flying to Jamaica after her stroke, I was greeted at the hospital by Chiney, Mama's devoted caregiver, who shared his concerns. I approached Mama's bedside for the first time since the stroke, the sight that greeted me was heart-wrenching. Her left side lay limp, her body rigid from immobility. She uttered no words, her recognition of me a mere flicker in her distant gaze. Though her smile upon my arrival conveyed a fleeting sense of awareness, it was clear that her cognitive faculties were slipping away.

Despite my nursing background, my expertise was in delivering babies, not stroke rehabilitation. Still, I had the fundamentals of training and intuition. I approached Mama's care with a blend of tenderness and determination, tenderly embracing her and initiating gentle massages and range of motion exercises for her extremities. She intermittently voiced discomfort—a reassuring sign of her lingering ability to communicate. I then decided to give her a bed bath to freshen her up. I was livid at what I saw as I began to bathe her. Mere days into her hospital stay, there were already blisters marring her heels and coccyx. This wasn't merely a patient in need of care; it was my beloved Mama, and such substandard treatment was unacceptable. If the staff couldn't provide the care she deserved, I was determined to do it.

Each day, I dutifully attended her bedside, administering massages and exercises with unwavering devotion. Encouraging her to bear weight on her legs, I provided the crucial early interventions essential for stroke recovery. Amidst the routine of rehabilitation, I injected moments of levity, knowing the healing power of laughter. Silly dances, exaggerated imitations of church worshippers—anything to elicit a smile or a flicker of amusement from her. Though she seemed indifferent, I could sense her silent appreciation.

In fleeting moments of lucidity, Mama's questions revealed fragments of her awareness. She inquired what I was doing to her and I explained. I asked her if she knew who I was. Her responses offered glimpses into her perception of me. In her eyes, I had become synonymous with comfort and care— the bringer of "nice things." Though she seldom uttered my name, her recognition of my role, however veiled, marked a subtle yet significant progression in her communication. And so, in the quiet moments of our shared struggle, amidst the labyrinth of her fading consciousness, I found solace in the simple affirmation of our connection.

When we were young, my mother loved to have her hair combed. My sister Althea always did it for her, and Mama would smile and even hum because she enjoyed it so much. She'd often asked my sister to comb her hair even when her hair didn't need combing. This ritual was like a massage that relaxed her, and Althea (who has two sons, Joshua, and Mathew whom she took to Jamaica every year to see their grandma) has since shared with me that it was a deep affirmation of their love for each other and something she would deeply miss.

For some reason, I never cared for combing Mama's hair. I don't like to do other people's hair in general. When I was little, Mama always wanted me to comb and braid hers, which was thick and natural. I used to hide when she'd call out for me before bedtime. I knew what she wanted, and I didn't want to do it. But things changed once she got sick. I still didn't enjoy combing people's hair, but it brought her joy, so I did it without hesitation. While massaging her head, I'd gently run a comb through her hair. After a short time, I could hear her breathing becoming steadier and her body relaxed. Though she didn't know who I was, she enjoyed the ritual. I suppose it simply felt good and looking back, I realized Althea was right. It was a connection to her children, and it must have felt like a meditation to her. In that moment, I wanted to hug her with all my might. However, I knew that was what I needed and not necessarily what her fragile body could handle.

One morning I went in to see her, and I was wearing a yellow and black outfit with a scarf.

"Oh, pretty, very pretty," she said.

"Oh yeah, you like bright colors, I remember." I cajoled.

"Yes, I do," she answered as she nodded her head.

"And your favorite color is red," I said and she smiled.

"Yes, yes, it is."

It was true, my mom loved reds, oranges, and yellows, and she loved wearing bright colors. That was the moment she started coming around and talking more. It solidified my wavering faith. When her movements improved, I asked the doctor to release her from the hospital. I thought she could get more love and better care at home. However, she had to stay put until she could drink or eat without the feeding tube. Before long, I was giving her sips of coconut water, and she was enjoying it without difficulty. Soon she was gulping down a bottle of Ensure like she was starving. I got excited and told the nurse, and they started making arrangements to send her home.

Mama's discharge coincided with my departure for the States, a bittersweet development compounded by a disheartening revelation. The hospital had slated her physical therapy for March—four months away. The gravity of the situation weighed heavily on me. I knew all too well the critical window for stroke rehabilitation. Every passing hour without therapy risked irreversible deterioration—a prospect too dire to contemplate. Despite my resolve, the stark reality was that Jamaica lacked the required facilities, and transporting Mama to California was impractical and unwise. Caught in a bind, torn between familial obligations and geographical constraints, I entrusted her care to Chiney and a hired nurse's aide, giving them detailed instructions and expectations. Friends and family served as vigilant guardians of Mama's well-being in my absence.

As I boarded the plane bound for Los Angeles my heart was heavy with the weight of separation Then a phone call came from the nurse with good news: Mama, with steadfast determination, had risen from her wheelchair with only a little help to walk from the car to her house. The news washed over me like a benediction, dispelling the doubt that lingered in my mind. I held my tears at bay, clinging to the promise of Mama's resilience. It was the divine intervention I desperately sought, a beacon of light illuminating the path ahead as I reluctantly embarked on my journey back to the United States.

Mama's will and determination showed up one more time. I think they made her defy her doctor when he said she would never walk again. It wouldn't have surprised me if Mama had fully recovered. "Oh, you think I'm gone?" I could easily imagine her saying. "I'm not dead yet." She'd smirk and give her 'under the eye' look.

I've come to understand the formidable power of the mind and the unwavering strength of faith. It's a revelation that transcends the confines of logic, affirming the age-old adage that faith can indeed move mountains. Mama lived by the creed that if one can conceive and believe, one can achieve—a mantra now etched into the fabric of my being. Yet, she also imparted the wisdom that there comes a time when we must surrender to the divine will and entrust our fate to higher forces. I find solace in the belief that Mama's journey, however it unfolded was guided by the hand of God. Even if it meant relinquishing her to the embrace of eternity rather than watching her endure further suffering, I prayed for the wisdom to accept His will with grace and fortitude.

With many of her contemporaries and her two eldest children deceased, Mama, who'd done so much for her community of Corn Piece, would now need to rely on others to care for her. With all her remaining daughters abroad, her remaining son mentally ill, and an ailing husband at home, I had to decide on Mama's long-term care moving forward. It was time. Though Mama had said to rely on faith, we all knew some changes had to be made. We needed a trustworthy caregiver who understood her disease. This was an essential part of the quality care she needed to receive going forward. Chiney, a true ally, had been caring for Mama and her husband. He was very dedicated but not knowledgeable about this kind of care, and it wouldn't be fair for him to shoulder the burden and unpredictability that came with it.

I, too, was unprepared for all the changes and the end-of-life considerations that needed to be handled. With Mama's rapid decline, it was too late to go through the long-drawn-out and potentially volatile process of which family members and advisors should be in charge. To make matters worse, Mama's third husband was also infirmed. He'd had children from his first marriage, but they were not involved in his care, so the responsibility for both of them landed squarely on my shoulders. In addition, we needed to care for our Danny since Mama was still his primary caregiver.

"Who will take care of Danny?" was one of Mama's biggest worries when she realized she was losing herself.

Alzheimer's is unforgiving. Like a thief, it robs years of memories, wiping life's slate clean. It was heart-wrenching to watch Mama's powerful mind slip away and her body grow frail. Mama, always a very private person, especially with her businesses, had been closed-lipped about her affairs. I, as her executor, had records, but I wanted to take advantage of her lucid moments to sort out her affairs with her help. I only hoped I had all the information I'd need to set things straight.

And the worst was yet to come. During her final decline, Mama was diagnosed with an abdominal aortic aneurysm, an enlargement of the abdominal aorta. I knew what this meant, and I steeled myself for the outcome. I spoke to the doctors, did my research, and decided it was not in Mama's best interest, especially in her fragile state, to move forward with surgery. As a healthcare professional, I knew that prolonging life, even my mother's, is not always the right thing to do.

I also knew that having such invasive surgery at such an advanced age and in her current condition would not have been her choice. Mama wouldn't even have dental surgery. I remember once when she was in California, I took her to get custom-fitted dentures. Mama hated every moment of it, and as soon as they began to feel uncomfortable, she stopped wearing them altogether. I then suggested she get permanent replacement teeth. Mama flat-out refused. She'd rather be toothless!

However, Judith, who'd not communicated with our mother for some time, wanted to move ahead with the surgery. I was not happy with the decision. To appease her, I listened to and observed the wishes of my sister who'd somehow convinced Mama's husband that she should have the surgery. But I made it clear that I would not be responsible for the outcome. In the end, after evaluating Mama, the anesthesiologist advised, "If we do this, she'll probably never come off the respirator."

I'm glad he spoke up because he was able to change the surgeon, Judith, and Mama's husband's minds.

Unfortunately, medical care had gotten to a place where money was a huge consideration in Jamaica. As far as the medical administrative facility was concerned, it was just money in their pocket. They were neither invested in Mama's survival nor her aftercare; it was just another costly procedure that inflated their success data. For me it is about the quality of my mother's life *after* surgery. Bedridden, stiff with blisters and bedsores, was probably what she'd have to look forward to. This was not my idea of a peaceful death. This was not the end-of-life experience I wanted for my mother. If I knew anything about my mother, determined as she was, I knew she would never muster the strength to recover. She was eighty-one, in full-blown Alzheimer's with an abdominal aneurysm. She knew her time was near, and dementia or not, I know for sure she would prefer to go with the dignity with which she had lived her life.

That issue resolved, we now had to deal with her estate. Mama was a wealthy woman by her rights and certainly by Jamaican standards. Equally true is that people's true colors are on full display when money is in the mix. Family members were now posturing and jockeying for positions to control Mama's estate. Feelings were hurt, loved ones began acting out, and relationships fractured, became strained, cantankerous or downright nonexistent.

I'm not one to be in the fray. Everyone dealing with the imminent loss of Mama was behaving badly enough on their own, and we were all adjusting to the coming change. The duplicity of false friends who professed their loyalty to Mama added fuel to the fire. Though I was the executor of Mama's will, with Gem gone there was only one other person whom Mama had trusted with her day-to-day affairs, Mrs. Stewart. She was a Justice of the Peace (Notary Public) and the principal of my alma mater. She had been acting as Mama's real estate manager and confidant and collecting monies from her various land sales and rental properties, and should have been paying Mama's tax bills.

One day, when I was visiting my mom, she was restless and wanted me to visit Mrs. Stewart. In a lucid moment, Mama told me that she'd been asking Mrs. Stewart for her money for more than a year without any success. She further stated Mrs. Stewart might have been out of the country at one point which was confirmed. She wanted me to go with her to visit Mrs. Stewart at her school to see if we could shame her into paying the monies owed for the properties she'd bought from Mama, as well as other monies she was collecting from the sale of other properties. We went to see Mrs. Stewart in her office at Vere Technical High School. Mama introduced me as her daughter from America. Mrs. Stewart was quite polite and knew exactly who I was, reminding me she'd called me in the States to tell me I needed to come and help my mom.

As I understood it, for more than a few years, Mama had been asking her, "What happened, man? When are you going to give me *suppen*?" Mrs. Stewart told Mama to come back in a few days. When we returned a few days later, she gave us JA$ 30,000 dollars in cash a mere pittance of the monies owed and promised to start paying JA$30,000 per month. We came to suspect that Mrs. Stewart might have been robbing Mama. We received only two other payments and never received any funds from the American who supposedly purchased land from my mother that she was collecting. This made my mom sad.

It was alleged that Mrs. Stewart had been collecting money from another landowner for Mama in American dollars but not giving it to her. True or not, it was heart-wrenching to think that someone Mama trusted and held in high esteem and who knew my mom was compromised with a debilitating disease would violate her trust. To steal from her 'beloved' friend, alleged or not, was disturbing. I remember Mama saying to her, "If I find out you were not honest with me, I will cry." I felt the sadness and disappointment of my mother as we sat in Mrs. Stewart's office at Vere Technical High School.

I'd had my own share of disappointment with Mrs. Stewart. I'd wanted to donate some money to the track students on the relay team that year I was in Jamaica. There was a track meet and I'd committed US$50.00 each to the runners on the winning girl's 4X100 relay team, plus their alternates. Mrs. Steward approved the contribution and so I gave her US$250.00 for the five students. As principal, she authorized the gift. After she received the money I went to the track meet, only now she informed me that the students were not allowed to accept cash so she bought them a gift basket each. I could not believe it. The most each of those baskets could have cost was ten to fifteen U.S. dollars. I was disappointed, to say the least, and knew then I was not dealing with an honest broker. I knew what my mother was feeling even in her state of dementia was correct.

I often say you can tell a person's character by how they treat the vulnerable, and if blessed, how they share their resources. Mama wanted to succeed not only for herself but also for her community and shared her resources with her people. How could this woman in such a position have done this to her friend and confidant? I was utterly stunned and disgusted.

Having carried the weight of the past three years, it was difficult to engage with family members who decided to have issues, and my sister Judith was leading the disruptive pack. Being in charge of Mama's care for them meant managing her resources and they wanted theirs. Their displeasure should not have been the least of my concern, but at that time it was very stressful and disheartening.

Gem would have handled this with finesse. But I'm not Gem, nor do I have her temperament. Now that I had to deal with the challenges before me without her support, I steeled myself with Mama's non-negotiable qualities. I was determined to carry out her wishes, honoring the specific principles by which she lived. More than anything I wanted to ensure everything was done with the purest of intentions and according to Mama's requests for her and for Gem.

I wanted no regrets about my mother's care as she approached the end of her life. I shifted my full attention to her life, knowing I could move forward with my own once she was well cared for. So, again, I left my affairs in California to be with my mother. It was radical and emotionally costly but I was very comfortable with it, and there was no question who had my heart at that moment.

As the challenging times unfolded, I began to learn more about who I was, where I was going, and the why of my own life. One has to be content with themselves to truly be happy with another. Mama had been content with herself. That's why she could love Papa even with his frailties. That's why she loved Brother Ford and Brother Miller. She loved herself, and therefore, she could love because to love another person in their imperfection is to love yourself with yours. I needed to commit to loving myself before fully committing to having the perfect love in my life.

My earlier loves may not have survived my dedication to my family, which was okay because today I'm happy and fulfilled *because* I gave the loves of my life—my brother, sister, and mother—the very best of me. I am happy and grateful their spirits live in me, and I'm full of love. My bucket runneth over because of the people who loved me. I believe in love and its power, and I continue to live it to this day! I believe that when I am ready, true love will find me, that is if it's God's will—just like Mama always taught me. I also learned that it didn't matter what anyone thought of me as long as I knew I did the right things for the right reasons. My authenticity and true intentions might make people love me, but they may not and that's alright.

I'd built a sustainable business that could run without me and so I was able to spend as much time as possible when Mama passed. If I couldn't take time to be with my mother in her last days, what would be the good of all she had given me?

At first, I shuffled back and forth. It was challenging but I got used to it. Unfortunately, reality dictated that I couldn't be with Mama in perpetuity as things needed my attention at home. While back in California on one of my trips, I felt the need for a more permanent solution. I had to find someone reliable for Mama, someone who would give me peace of mind. I needed help finding such a caregiver, but it was hard to trust anyone already in the mix with all the ongoing hullabaloos. Mama would say, "Put your faith in God to deliver the right person." And I did. I prayed for someone empathetic who understood the aberrant behavior of Alzheimer's patients and who was genuinely loving and kind.

As they say, God works in mysterious ways. One day out of the blue, I got a call from one of my very good friends Elaine (Patsy) Beckford with whom I'd lost touch over the years. I'd always wished I could find her again, and here she was calling. As with good friends, we just picked up where we left off as though time had evaporated. While we were catching up, I expressed my deep concern for Mama and my wish to find a reliable caregiver. It had to be a woman because Mama was at that stage where she needed female support, and Chiney needed reliable, intelligent help. All caught up, we ended our conversation, and promised to keep in touch.

The next day, I received a call from Elaine with an offer. She would help! My girlfriend, Elaine Patsy Beckford, was a blessing from God. I had always practiced visualization in my young life, but as I got older, I fully came to appreciate the power of the mind in manifesting goodness and blessings. This was something I knew Mama practiced and yet another lesson I'd learned. Immediately I felt freer. My friend was back in my life, and in such a significant way. One week later, Elaine was on a plane from Canada to care for Mama in Jamaica. I was happy and grateful, and my tears flowed as freely as I felt. Indeed, she was a real blessing. She spent three months with Mama. I couldn't have wished for more.

I relaxed somewhat, although I was aware of what was to come.

I prepared to go through the grieving process. And on August 25, 2013, the inevitable arrived. The circle of life closed its loop for my mother. Within a few weeks of Elaine's return to her own life, Mama passed. It was exactly two weeks after her husband died. I'd been with her those two weeks prior when he passed. Mama always said she would never bury another husband, and here it was, she'd gotten her wish. I believe that when Brother Miller left, it gave Mama the permission she needed to follow him.

I was at the park with my youngest sister Althea when Chiney called with the news. I felt lost and sad, but to be honest, it was a relief that she would no longer ail. I was expecting it. Still, though I knew it was near, I didn't want to accept it. My mother's life on earth had ended. It was a sobering experience. I went numb, but no tears would fall. I had to hold it together. I had to be strong until the very end.

When Mama passed away, I wanted to celebrate her extraordinary life with gratitude and a free heart, knowing that I'd done all I could in this life to give back to the woman who gave me life.

I went into turbo mode. The one thing I took comfort in was knowing that I'd done everything in my power to make sure Mama and her husband's end of life was as dignified and as comfortable as possible.

I flew back to Jamaica to plan for Mama's homegoing. Because of brewing contention, I chose not to go to our family home where the others were staying, I spent the time with the Dyers in Montego Bay where my girlfriend Odette and I planned and coordinated the service. The night before the funeral, I moved to a hotel near our home for the wake. That night at the wake or 'set-up' as it is called in Jamaica, a celebration of Mama's life, I spared no expense for a lavish celebration with food, drink, and song to celebrate Mama's life.

The place was packed to the gills with people, all regaling us with tales of Mama. I was especially glad that Danny was there as he'd been distraught and agitated. Having had Mama as his caregiver for years, Danny couldn't accept that she was gone. "Is Mama gone?" he kept repeating, his face blank. His sadness was heartfelt and it brought sadness to my heart. "Is Mama really gone?"

Danny refused to attend the funeral the following day. He just couldn't. It would have been too final. Danny and Mama had grown very close. I remember a story of a burglar breaking into the house in Mama's room. Danny pulled out the machete and some acid, doused the person, and said, "Get out man, that's my mother get out." And the criminal took off. He was always protective of his Mama.

The setup night did not go off completely without a hitch. My sister Judith was on the warpath. Uncooperative with all the decisions being made, I learned that she'd told everyone at the wake that there would be no funeral, and that therefore, this night was the celebration of Mama's life. I refused to engage. I wanted to keep the focus on the sendoff for my mom. Thanks to all my big beautiful male cousins, Aunt Mavis' clan, who loved their auntie and who had my back, I was able to keep the peace. One reason for Judith's anger was that we'd chosen to bury Mama in the family plot with her mother and father instead of on the land Mama's father had given her. Aunt Mavis had passed on five months earlier, and both she and Aunt Girty were buried on their plots. Judith kept insisting that all Mama's sisters were buried in their plots, so why couldn't Mama be in hers?

However, because Mama had had three husbands, I decided to bury her on the family plot. It was discussed with mom on numerous occasions and she was alright with it. No one objected but Judith, who'd put on quite a dramatic show of defiance. I'd been caring for Mama and her husband since Gem left us three years before. I was annoyed that she wouldn't see fit to give me the benefit of the doubt. I decided to take the high road as I've never been one to engage in a certain battle, even as a child.

The day of the funeral was a God-given Jamaican day to send off Mama. It was simply heavenly. Jamaican people go to funerals whether or not they know the deceased, and for as much as my mother had done for her community, I had expected her funeral to be overflowing. Expecting many people, including some dignitaries from the church, in addition to the church members and other community folks, we erected a tent outside with audiovisual equipment to accommodate any overflow traffic. Though there was standing room only in the church, to my surprise and utter disappointment the tent remained partially empty. My hope that the Ministers and dignitaries Mama had entertained at our home, especially since I was Honorary Consul to Jamaica in Los Angeles at the time, might have shown up did not materialize. One of the ministers did bring words as the government representative of the then Prime Minister, Portia Simpson. It was a lesson in expectations. One that Mama had already taught, but I'd forgotten.

I wondered if Judith's behavior the night before had kept people away. Still, it was a beautiful service. The minister was robust and expressive. A special singer came who lit the room on fire. My cousin Carmen was chosen by the family to do the eulogy and her delivery was heartfelt. My cousin Horace, one of Mama's favorite nephews could not attend because of his religious beliefs, as the service was held on Saturday, his Sabbath. Althea and I gave remarks. Althea's extemporaneous speech was earnest and moving. Judith arrived late, did not speak but had another dramatic moment at the end of the service. It was unfortunate that she would bring this kind of chaos to her mother's homegoing. She caused issues later as well, demanding the reading of the Will right after the repast, and even praised Mrs. Stewart, who in my opinion, had not served my mother well in the end, to put it mildly.

True to my mother's unwavering sense of duty and compassion, she had meticulously arranged for each of her children to have their own bank account early in our lives. I chose to leave the inevitable familial tensions and turmoil that ensued behind in Jamaica. With the steadfast support of my friends and confidants, including the indefatigable Patsy and my ever-reliable friend, Odette Dyer, who stood by my side as we navigated the tribulations with unwavering resolve, I held my head high. I had fulfilled the solemn promise I made to myself—I had honored my mother's legacy and stood poised to extend her wisdom not only to our kin but to the wider world, where her guidance is sorely needed. In the tradition of our

African ancestors, who passed down their legacies through oral narratives, I understood that the endurance of legends lies in the retelling of their stories.

As the sun dipped below the horizon in a blaze of orange-red hues reminiscent of the very shade my mother adored, her celectial crown adorned with stars, each representing a soul she had guided towards the path of righteousness it signified her ascension into the celestial embrace of the spiritual realm. I felt a profound sense of peace wash over me. I knew then that my mother was being welcomed home.

Though my heart remained stoic, shielded by a veil of numbness at the realization that I would no longer see my mother in the flesh, I resolved to return home. The tears I could not shed at the moment of her passing were a testament to the depth of my grief and the magnitude of my loss. Yet, as I reflect on my journey with her, I am filled with a profound sense of contentment. I loved her, and she loved me. I am my mother's daughter, entrusted with one of the sacred baton of her legacy, which I carry forth with pride. This narrative of my life with My Mother, My Champion, ensures that her spirit lives on, offering her wisdom to those who seek it.

WORKBOOK

This 'praise, the bridge that carries you over' story of my mother's life lessons, proved a guiding light to the life I constructed for myself. I've worked with many young people throughout the years, and my work as a mentor has been one of the most rewarding things I've done. Many do not have the benefit of a parent to hold their space, so put as a part of the village that will raise them, I wanted to pass on some of the valuable lessons my mother passed on to me.

In true Afro-Caribbean style, we tell the stories of the past so the future can have a footprint as a guide for those to come to follow.

The workbook offers exercises for self-discovery and tips of tried and proven methodologies that are the bedrock of a successful life no matter in what field, to what race or creed; these are universal principles.

Chapter 1
Mama's Life Lessons:

- *Know who you are at your core. Are you a leader? A follower? Know your strengths and your weakness equally well.*
- *Ask yourself: are you an outlier? Been told you don't fit the norm? Brilliant, sharp, and colorful minds are the change agents of the world.*
- *Always maintain unwavering strength and faith in something or someone greater than you—they will steer you through darkness and act as a beacon of light.*
- *Stay true to your values and let them radiate and shining bright.*

Self-Reflection Exercise # 1

Are you a leader or a follower?

What are your strengths?

_____

_____

_____

_____

_____

_____

_____

_____

What are your weaknesses?

_____

_____

_____

_____

_____

_____

_____

_____

_____

What is your superpower?

What is your why? Your purpose? Do you really know?

Chapter 2
Mama's Life Lessons:

- *Don't be afraid to dream*
- *Surround yourself with people who believe in your dreams*
- *Turn a deaf ear to those who can't see your vision even as you accept their limitations.*
- *Don't give in to fear. Fear is nothing but False Evidence Appearing Real. You are real not fear. Fear is excitement without the breath, so take a few deep breaths and move forward.*

Self-Reflection Exercise # 2

What limiting beliefs do you maintain in your life? How have they affected your efforts?

What would be your legacy if you acted on your dreams without fear? What history would you like to leave.

If you left the world today, how would you want to be remembered?

Who have you met in your life that left the greatest impression upon you? Why?

Chapter Three
Mama's Life Lessons:

- *Love is the greatest gift you can give and receive.*
- *Be proud to share your loved ones with others. They are simply a reflection of your best features.*
- *Treat all people as if they were royalty. Everyone deserves the best you have to offer.*
- *Keep your eyes on the small things in life. Often, the details make the difference.*
- *Caring for others is an asset, not a liability.*
- *Take every opportunity in life to make others smile.*

Self-Reflection Exercise # 3

Have you experienced love in any way? If not, what can you do to find the love inside of you?

If you have experienced love in any way, how you pay it forward?

_____

_____

_____

_____

_____

_____

_____

_____

Are there people in your life who could benefit from a giving hand?

_____

_____

_____

_____

_____

_____

_____

_____

171

Who are the people you are most proud of in your life? Why?

Chapter 4
Mama's Life Lessons:

- *Setbacks are a part of a life well lived.*
- *Every adversity brings with it the seed of an equivalent advantage*
- *Good things come from bad situations if you just change your point of view.*
- *Always be aware. Pay attention to what's around you. You never know when a door might open that will make a difference in your life.*

Self-Reflection Exercise # 4

What is your general attitude and reaction when you fall short of your goals?

_____

_____

_____

_____

_____

_____

_____

_____

_____

_____

What lessons did you learn when fell short of your goals?

_____

_____

_____

_____

_____

_____

_____

_____

_____

What ways tools and strategies will you implement to pick yourself up after a setback?

_____

_____

_____

_____

_____

_____

_____

_____

How can you change your perception and opinion about a seemingly negative situation?

Chapter 5
Mama's Life Lessons:

- *Inspire others to greatness by doing good deeds.*
- *Be a positive member of your community by helping others.*
- *Joy comes from the simplest things; a smile, a walk in the garden; a chat with a friend.*
- *Know when to talk, but more importantly, know when to listen.*
- *It is the little acts in life that show others you care.*

Self-Reflection Exercise # 5

What do you do to find joy every day?

What do you do to bring joy to others?

_____

_____

_____

_____

_____

_____

_____

_____

_____

How often do you spend each day listening to others?

_____

_____

_____

_____

_____

_____

_____

_____

_____

Do you belong to a community? What about community inspires you?

Are you a good listener?

Chapter 6
Mama's Life Lessons:

- *Family is the most important thing in life; always be there to support and care for those you love.*
- *Never give up on the ones you love, even when the going gets tough.*
- *Never judge a person for their shortcomings. We all have obstacles we must overcome.*

Self-Reflection Exercise # 6

How do you prioritize the people you love?

What lessons have you learned from your family elders?

_____

_____

_____

_____

_____

_____

_____

When was the last time you gave up on someone you love? What compelled you to do so?

_____

_____

_____

_____

_____

_____

_____

_____

Chapter 7
Mama's Life Lessons:

- *Work never killed anyone, but being lazy will.*
- *Don't expect anything to be handed to you. You have to earn every inch.*
- *You can achieve anything you want, but it comes with hard work*
- *Attitude equals Altitude.*

Self-Reflection Exercise # 7

What's your attitude toward life and others? Positive? Negative?

Where did your attitude to life come from?

If success is 10 % inspiration and 90% perspiration, how do you sustain your drive for the long haul?

*Look around you. Who are the people you surround yourself with.
Strivers, doers or otherwise?*

Chapter 8
Mama's Life Lessons:

- *Education is the bedrock of progress*
- *Education comes in all forms, formal and informal*
- *Common Sense is priceless*

Self-Reflection Exercise # 8

What is your aspiration toward education?

What is your aspiration toward lifelong learning?

Are you aware of the services available to you for furthering your education?

Chapter 9
Mama's Life Lessons:

- *Look for the little signs that show us the biggest changes.*
- *Trust your instincts and intuition. They are often more enlightening than you think.*
- *Know when to stand your ground and when it is more important to walk away.*

Self-Reflection Exercise # 9

Do you listen to your gut feeling?

Can you read a room? Do you know when it's time to speak up and when silence speaks volumes? Can you give an example of when you did this? How did it make you feel?

Are you observant? Do you notice the small efforts that yield big results? Give an example.

Do you have clear boundaries regarding what you will and will not tolerate?

Chapter 10
Mama's Life Lessons:

- *Spiritual relationships are everlasting.*
- *Faith makes you strong and successful.*
- *If you can conceive it and believe it, you can achieve it.*
- *Faith will keep you going through the darkest of times.*
- *Know your values and morals.*

Self-Reflection Exercise # 10

What role if any does spirituality play in your life?

What is your definition of faith?

Do you believe faith impacts our values, hopes, and dreams? Why or why not?

_____

_____

_____

_____

_____

_____

_____

_____

Have you ever experienced something that required belief in something bigger than yourself?

_____

_____

_____

_____

_____

_____

_____

_____

Morally or ethically speaking, do you know the line in your life you will never cross?

Chapter 11
Mama's Life Lessons:

- *Know when to let go.*
- *How you respond to illness matters.*
- *Always strive for empathy*

Self-Reflection Exercise # 11

What difficult situations have you experienced in your life? Have you ever had to cut your losses in difficult situations?

Do you consider yourself to be a nurturing person? Why or why not?

Have you ever extended yourself to someone in need? If so why? If not why?

Chapter 12
Mama's Life Lessons:

- *Practice self-care. The rest will follow.*
- *Take care of those who care for you.*
- *Not everyone will support you. Those who matter will always be there when you need them.*

Self-Reflection Exercise # 12

- *Do you take your health for granted?*

- *What do you do to make sure you are in optimum mental and physical shape?*

- *Is your life stress-free or stressful? What will you do about it?*

- *When was the last time you took a vacation?*

- *Do you feel you have a balance between your professional life and personal life? Why or why not?*

_____

_____

_____

_____

_____

_____

_____

_____

- *Do you have a support system both in your personal and work life?*

_____

_____

_____

_____

_____

_____

_____

_____

_____

What are your strongest character traits?

Chapter 13
Mama's Life Lessons

- *Constantly evaluate life and look for areas of improvement.*
- *Share your success with others*

Self-Reflection Exercise # 13

What did you learn about yourself from these exercises?

_____

_____

_____

_____

_____

_____

_____

_____

_____

_____

_____

_____

How will you implement these lessons into your everyday life?

Where do you see yourself in ten years?

If your journey has been fulfilling, how will you pay it forward?

ACKNOWLEDGMENTS

The list of people I need to acknowledge is long, but I want to take the time to say thank you because no one goes it alone. I want each of you to know how grateful I am for your support and for you being a part of my life's journey, and an important part of my mother's life. Thank you. Elaine (Pansy) Beckford: You are the definition of love, care, and friendship, a true servant of God. Thank you for the tender loving care you gave to my mother and me. Priceless! Chiney: For all you have done for my mother, the woman who raised you. A special thank you for picking up where Mama left off with Danny. My dear friend Odette Dyer: thank you for being there with me every step of the way. I couldn't have done it without you. Thanks to Mr. Dyer. My brother Danny who suffers from mental illness and drug addiction, may God bless you and heal you. Just know that you are loved and I'm doing all I can to keep you safe and well. I love you and I hope you can feel my love. Mama is watching over you. To my sister Judith: Our journey has been challenging. Mama taught us throughout her life example that Family is first. I love you. To my baby sister Althea: You'll always be my baby sister; strong, beautiful, and smart. To Joshua and Matthew, Mama loved you, keep her memories alive. Roderick, thank you for all your support.

Lor-ren my niece, you will always be the baby my sister, Gem, had for me and I know will carry on Mama's legacy. Luke and Samuel will know her through you. My cousin, Horace Mason (Slippy,) a brother, mentor, and cheerleader, your sudden death has left a void in my life. When Gem left I had you, now you are gone and I will have to figure it out on my own now. R.I.P. Brother Miller, Mama's husband a posthumous thank you for the beautiful years you gave to each other, R.I.P. To Aunt Mavis: Your husband (Johnny) Lester Moulton taught me as a young child about philanthropy before I could say the word. Thank you for being an integral part of my growing up, you are both missed. RIP. To the children and cousins to whom Mama taught the true meaning of family, I love you all to the moon and back.

To Brother Ormsby: I know you are with Mama again, RIP. Alester Palmer (Ali P. Aunt Girty's son): You have handled many of Mama's finances like a champ. I wish love and blessings to you, Carol, and the rest of your family. Thank you for helping with my little brother Danny's care—Mama sees you. And your brother Tony, Mama loved you cuz and I love you too. To Nikiesha: Mama's most remembered grandchild in the end.

To Sassy: one of the first to notice that she was forgetting things and encouraged me to take action. To Bryan: Thanks for all you did for Mama. Mama loved you. To my cousin Mark Moulton (Robin) my Aunt Mavis's eldest son, who help me to fill in some of the family's blank memories and history. Whenever I asked questions about the family history everyone would say ask Robin because his mom shared it all with him. He is our family encyclopedia or I guess I should say our Google. To all the grandchildren who grew up in America and never got to know your grandmother, you have missed a beautiful and powerful soul who will live on through you and in me forever. To Vinnette Smith, my childhood friend and daughter of Evangelist Smith who helped me fill in some of my blank memories of our mother's journey. June Carryl thank you for reading my manuscript and providing valuable feedback. Your approval means the world to me. Peggy McColl - Canada and Valerie Facey - Jamaica: Thank you both for all you have done to inspire me to write this book. Your guidance and encouragement have been a blessing along this tough yet loving journey.

ABOUT THE AUTHOR

Lorna Mae Johnson, a dynamic trailblazer who has transformed lives and shattered ceilings is the embodiment of the American dream. From her roots in Jamaica, through Canada, to the United States, Lorna's journey is a testament to resilience and ambition.

A former Olympic-level athlete, Lorna sprinted alongside legends like Evelyn Ashford, Alice Brown, and the late Florence Griffith Joyner (Flo-Jo) at the Mt. SAC Relays. This athletic prowess was just the beginning of her multifaceted career.

Transitioning from the track to healthcare, Lorna initially trained as a registered nurse. She then earned a Master of Science in Nurse-Midwifery and Finance from the University of Southern California, graduating with top honors in Phi Kappa Phi and Sigma Theta Tau, alongside a BSc in Healthcare Management.

Her entrepreneurial spirit led her to become a serial real estate investor and the founder of the LMJ Global Foundation (formerly Compassion for Teen Life), which promotes healthy lifestyles and education for low-income children worldwide. As the CEO of AFC Management Company and CFO of AFC Medical Group, she provides vital maternal and child healthcare services to underserved communities in East Los Angeles.

Lorna's leadership extends to numerous prestigious roles. Appointed by Supervisor Hilda Solis to the Los Angeles County Commission for Women, she champions the empowerment of women and girls. She's a council member of the White House Historical Association and has served on the President's Advisory Committee on the Arts at The John F. Kennedy Center for the Performing Arts under Presidents Obama and Biden. She also, as surrogate, played a significant role in the Hillary for America campaign and Chair for President Biden's Inaugural Committee.

Honored as one of the "Seven Wonder Women of the World" by Investing In Women and crowned as a Queen Mother in Ghana, Lorna's impact is global. She's the former President of the Florence-Firestone Chamber of Commerce and a clinical professor and lecturer at UCLA. Her efforts extend to the UN Foundation for Women and Girls and as the Honorary Consul of Jamaica in Los Angeles.

Lorna is a globally sought-after speaker on women's issues, financial literacy, and health education. She sponsors educational programs in Los Angeles, Malawi, and Jamaica and partners with Olympic medalist Alice Brown to nurture young athletic talent in Africa.

With a life dedicated to breaking barriers and uplifting others, Lorna Mae Johnson continues to inspire and lead, embodying the limitless possibilities of the American dream.

www.ingramcontent.com/pod-product-compliance
Lightning Source LLC
Chambersburg PA
CBHW061149120626
46546CB00005B/1991